M.J. AMHERST

THE STORIES I'LL TELL

A CONFESSIONAL COLLEGE ROMANCE ABOUT MESSY LOVE AND SELF-DISCOVERY

Jover Books

Distributed by Jover Books

ISBN: **979-8-90329-365-0** Paperback

ISBN: **979-8-90329-368-1** E-book

Dedication

This is for the attempt. For the glorious, imperfect, trembling first step into the fog. For believing there might be a dawn on the other side, even when you can't see it. For the brave. Not the unafraid, but those who feel the fear and do it anyway. To the reader, about to turn the first page of an unknown tale. And to every soul who understands the same feeling in the story of their own life.

Contents

CHAPTER ONE

First Class

I arrived at York University ten minutes before the start of my first class for the semester. For breakfast, I was craving a bar of chocolate to tide me through the day. I knew it wasn't exactly the breakfast of champions, and that there was a chance I'll be late for class, but I was willing to risk it all for a delicious, pure bliss of cocoa sweetness. The vending machine was at the opposite wing of the building so I ran to the other end as if it was a 5k road race.

I slowed down my pace as I watched a tall, slender guy assess the curated selection of candies from top left to right, then all the way down to the bottom row. He looked smart and dignified wearing a pair of dark-framed eyeglasses, a black long-sleeved shirt and light-washed denim jeans.

Please just choose one already and move -- I'm just here for a Snickers bar! -- is what I wanted to yell at him, but instead, I waited patiently behind him for my turn. He crossed his arms between his chest and pondered some more. He then put his thumb below his chin like Steve Jobs plotting the next most innovative technology that would change the future.

I stood behind him as I took a glimpse of my watch. *Oh no! I'm officially late for my first day at Writing class.* I panicked and right away rummaged for change in my coin purse. I peeked through the magnificent glass-covered vessel standing proud like a portable Willy Wonka's Chocolate Factory. *Okay, I just need to find a dollar and seventy-five cents for my Snickers.*

By this time, I was getting anxious for not having any change to purchase my drug – this diabetes-inducing sugar-coated cocoa goodness. I unzipped my bag's inside pocket. *Nope. No change there... two nickels yes, a dollar and seventy-five cents? No dice!*

"I thought there's something here... C'mon," I whispered to myself, feeling defeated. All that running around and panicking were all for nothing. I knelt down putting my bag on the floor as I took out all of its contents one by one.

I searched the bottom of my bag like a raccoon ransacking a garbage can. *You know you're desperate when you keep searching for something you know isn't there.*

Taking my bag's lining, I turned it inside out hoping a dollar and seventy-five cents would magically appear before my eyes.

"Shit... nothing!" I mumbled to myself.

The guy standing by glanced at me. I flashed him with a warm but worried smile, embarrassed by my public display of desperation.

He smiled back at me.

"Do you need some change?" he asked. "Yeah, kinda," I mumbled back in embarrassment. I quickly put back all of my personal belongings inside my bag. *I need to get to class like right now.*

"I have some change. What do you want to get?" He looked serious and kind.

"Oh no, that's okay. Thanks anyways, I really appreciate it." I regretted saying those words right away.

"No, really. I can't decide which one I want anyway."

"Are you sure?" I asked politely.

"Yes, I'm sure, which one?"

"The Snickers"

"Ok, that's A-12, for $1.75."

He looked on as he took the exact change from his pocket. He pushed each coin into the vending machine slot and without double-checking his entry on the keypad, pushed the button for the final act.

We both watched as this contraption moved slowly to drop a bar of guess what - Mr. Big.

"Oops! I think I pressed A-13 instead of A-12, sorry about that", he took the Mr. Big chocolate bar from below and handed it to me.

"I have no more change – is this ok?"

"Totally fine, thank you so much! See you around? I've got to go to class and I'm kind of already late!"

I gratefully accepted the chocolate bar with a big smile and rushed to go to my class without looking back. I didn't even get the chance to ask for his name or give him more praise for his generosity. I was ten minutes late. No regrets, I still thought it was all worth it.

There were about fifty students inside. I was trying to look calm and collected while I searched for unoccupied seats in class.

Why is everyone so quiet? I thought to myself.

The only available seat in class was in the middle row sandwiched in between two comfortably seated male neighbors.

"Excuse me..." I awkwardly scooched by. "Thank you..." I mumbled not making any eye contact with anyone.

Everyone was looking at me, and was getting free entertainment watching the awkward latecomer disturb the peace and order in the room.

I managed to get to the open seat. I slowly placed my rickety old laptop, my brown leather bag, and finally my Mr. Big chocolate bar on the table. The silence was deafening. The professor was busy writing a bunch of course info and all other pertinent first day shenanigans. I took this opportunity to open my laptop and turn the power button on.

Ready to take my first notes, baby! My good old laptop took it upon itself to announce that it was still alive and kicking with a bong-like startup sound in full volume blast. *Beeennnn-nnnggggg...*

Okay, relax. A little disturbance won't hurt anyone. I discreetly glanced side-to-side to check if anyone in the room noticed that I was the source of the annoying sound. Nobody seemed to care. Everything was just peachy until my laptop fan started making an internal noise like a Boeing 777 airplane taking off on the runway.

Concerned neighbors within two-meter radius were giving me the "WHAT THE FUCK?" look.

"Sorry..." I whispered apologetically to everyone who heard the old plane-like noise situation. I slowly and gently closed my laptop as if it would reduce the inconvenience. The airplane takeoff sound continued. I swiftly opened the laptop and held the power button. It asked me if I wanted it to sleep, restart or shut down. *Is there an option to kill? No? Okay, then shut down.*

I got rid of the annoying sound and everyone was safe, for now. *I am so sorry Mac Daddy.* This is what I call my trusted, humble computer. Mac Daddy had been with me since high school, and we shared so many school projects, presentations, online shopping, viral videos, porn, torrent movie pirating, and Netflix together.

The professor was a soft-spoken, mid-thirties looking, petite woman with dark short hair. She instructed the class to group ourselves into three for our first assignment. Since nobody really knew anybody yet in the half hour that passed, she suggested that we form our group with our existing neighbors.

I looked to my right and there I saw a blue-eyed hipster-looking guy with a carefully manicured face beard. He nodded as if he approved of me being together with him in a group. As a non-verbal sign of acceptance, I glanced back with bulging wide smiley eyes.

"Hi, I'm Andy!" he radiated a very friendly tone and timbre in his voice.

"Emma." I smiled as I waved my hand.

Andy looked like he took fashion seriously even on a Monday eight-thirty writing class. He was wearing a blue cardigan on top of a crisp white collared shirt, skinny black jeans, ankle-high boots, and a leather *Prada* backpack.

On my left, as it turned out, was a ruggedly handsome, gorgeous hunk. He faced me with his right arm dangling behind the backrest of his chair.

"Wanna be in the same group?" Mr. Gorgeous eagerly looked for a response from Andy and me.

"Of course, gorgeous! We're so in!" Andy responded on behalf of both of us.

Mr. Gorgeous blushed, laughed it off, and turned his attention to me.

"I'm Mark, by the way." He shook my hand like a charismatic politician counting on my vote for Election Day.

"I'm Andy..." Andy slowly said his name trying to lock eyes with Mark.

"Emma..." I uttered quickly while admiring Mark's sparkling light brown eyes.

Mark was hot, but he acted like he didn't even know it. He was towering over most men in class standing over six feet tall. He looked laid-back wearing a dark long sleeve shirt that's slightly fitted on his lean body, paired with straight-cut jeans and black lace-up sneakers.

My Mr. Big chocolate bar caught my attention as my stomach crumbled of hunger. While what I wanted was Snickers, beggars can't be choosers. *I must have a little bite!*

I grabbed my chocolate bar, and as I was about to tear the wrapper, Andy interjected.

"Oh My God, Mr. Big! That's my favorite chocolate! Can we trade? I have a Snickers bar!" Andy unzipped his leather backpack and swung the chocolate bar right in front of my face.

"Sweet! I wanted to get Snickers anyway but ended up with Mr. Big so here you go!" I tossed the bar on Andy's desk.

Andy quickly grabbed his trade and slowly unwrapped his Mr. Big chocolate bar, locking eyes with Mark.

"Well, what can I say, I like my chocolates like I like my men – BIG." Andy exclaimed, following up with a wink.

"Well, don't let me disappoint you." Mark rejoined as he smilingly shook his head.

"Sorry, I know I can be such a flirt," Andy whispered to me as he flipped his imaginary long hair and let out a mischievous little chuckle. I couldn't help but laugh as I whispered back, "Well to be fair, about the big men, you and me both".

"Saucy!" Andy blurted out loud to my immediate embarrassment.

"I think we should probably exchange phone numbers and emails so we could keep in touch." Mark quickly interrupted.

We exchanged contact information as the class came to an end. On the first day of the semester, I found a handsome hunk and a hilarious fashionista.

CHAPTER TWO

It's a date

It's Friday afternoon and I was hanging out at Sophia's café enjoying my overpriced latte and mediocre banana nut muffin. It started pouring rain outside and I didn't have an umbrella, but I didn't care because I felt like sitting in that cozy café forever. My last class for the day was at two-thirty in the afternoon which left me an hour to kill. *I love to read and have a quiet time by myself with headphones on, amidst fifty other students seeking shelter from the rain.* Sophia's had an incredible ambient lighting from its enormous windows, complete with hanging plants, high ceilings, exposed beams and free Wi-Fi. I was breezing through Elizabeth Gilbert's "Eat. Pray. Love."

Gosh, it's such a rollercoaster of emotion, I'm hooked! Plus, I've never been anywhere but around the city, at least I can imagine what it's like to be her in the trifecta of her spiritual travel journey.

I received a text message on my phone.

'Hey, I like that book but hate the movie. Do you mind if I join you?'

I froze for a good five seconds as I looked up to see this tall attractive guy walking up to me. *Mark?!*

All of the ladies in the cafe swiveled their heads to take a glimpse of this magnificent work of art – like when a Victoria's Secret Supermodel walks into a room, but a fully clothed male version.

"Nice to see you here," as if answering my unspoken thought, "I'm glad we exchanged phone numbers in class. You seem so serious reading that book so I have to give you a breather. May I sit with you?"

"Of course, please."

Mark locked eyes with me, smiling coyly as he brushed his hair back with his right hand. He looked like an apparition of an angel.

"I love rainy days" I said coyly.

"Of course you do! It's the most romantic time to read about travelling the world in some cozy café, until some guy interrupts your precious alone time." Mark jokingly said as he raised his eyebrow.

I giggled like a little schoolgirl and felt myself begin to blush nervously.

"So, I assume you've read the book AND watched the movie since you gave it a mixed review." I taunted back at him.

"Yes, but only because I'm a Film Major and it was required in class."

"There's no shame in loving a Julia Roberts movie and picking up a woman's travel memoir while eating a tub of ice cream."

"Yeah, but I got really, really fat. So, I'm justified if I hate it." Mark rejoined.

We talked for an hour about nonsensical things and laughed at our silly banters. *I can't help but have a huge crush on him. But I shouldn't keep my hopes up. He's way out of my league and would never want someone like me.*

"So, there's this party tonight at my buddy's crib. Would you like to come?" Mark asked interrupting my thoughts.

What?! Is Mark inviting me to a house party? I haven't been out in a while. Of course, I want to go and hang out with him! Yes, Yes, Yes!!!! Oh no!!! – I have a shift at the diner tonight.

"Uhm, I would like to, but I'm supposed to work at the diner tonight until closing time at ten." I meekly replied.

"The party doesn't start until ten at night."

"I see, but I don't have a car so I really can't. Maybe some other time?"

"I'll pick you up when you're done. C'mon, it's gonna be fun! My buddy Jay is a cool host and a DJ!"

"Okay, if it's not too much of a trouble to you."

"Alright, scoop you at 10 p.m. Which diner?

"Frankie's, on Main Street."

"It's a date! See you then!"

Uhm... Okay, did he say, It's a DATE??? Oh no, I don't have anything fancy *to wear in my bag to change in, other than my Frankie's diner outfit – black jeans, black long-sleeve blouse and black loafers. This ensemble looks more like a funeral attire. Good thing I have a decent camel trench coat that wraps around my body ala Parisian chic.* These thoughts raced through my mind as I went to my afternoon class giddy with excitement thinking about hanging out with Mark after work that night.

At five minutes before ten I rushed off to the restroom to apply some lipstick and blush. I finished the look by tying up my hair on a high bun for that I-made-an-effort look. I came out of the diner and found Mark leaning back on the driver's side outside his car.

"Ready to go? – you look great!" Mark mentioned as I blushed.

"I'm ready! Thanks for picking me up!" I smiled as he opened the front passenger door for me.

Mark played old-school alternative rock music throughout our car ride. We were jiving as we sang along to Joan Osborne's "One of Us"

'What if God was one of us? □

Just a slob like one of us' □

We breezed through traffic like we were on an impromptu car karaoke.

We got to Jay's house. His parents were totally cool with their only son hosting parties in their house. Their abode was equivalent to the size of three houses of an average family. They had a vast backyard with a pool, but his guests hung out in the basement which looked like a private posh club.

The basement had a fully stocked bar that could serve almost any drink in the world. The place was decorated with leather sofas, Moroccan poufs, and bar stools. There were about fifty people talking, dancing, and drinking. Jay played a mix of old and new hip hop when we arrived – the guests were a little buzzed and were at the peak mood to party. Mark and I sat by the bar. There's food laid out, catered in buffet style. I helped myself with a couple of sliders, a small portion of garden salad, and a bit of nachos.

Mark introduced me to Jay, and they began performing a secret handshake.

"Emma, I'll have to make a phone call. Will you be okay here for a minute?" said Mark.

"Yeah, absolutely."

"Emma, what's your favorite drink?" Jay asked as he went behind the bar.

"Uhm, a Mojito..."

"Alright you got it!"

"If you don't have mint..."

"No worries, I have everything I need to make your drink!"

Jay made the best mojito I've ever had in my life – served in a chilled tall glass with limes, fresh mint, soda water, white rum, sugar, and plenty of ice cubes.

"Oh My God! This is so good!" I gushed after taking a big sip.

"Thanks, glad you liked it!" Jay smiled as I practically gulped down the rest.

"Do you always throw awesome parties on a Friday night with a bunch of strangers?" I asked after finishing my mojito.

"Not every Friday night. But yeah, I like partying with strangers sometimes."

"Are you and Mark like best friends, or something?"

"Yeah, you can say that, we've known each other since we were six."

"Wow, that's a really long...." I forgot what I was going to say when I saw Mark come back walking towards us.

He's holding two bottles of Corona light.

"Did Jay tell you how long he's been planning this party?" chuckled Mark as he handed me a bottle of beer.

"Nah, we're just talking smack about you, bro!" Jay laughed as he walked towards his laptop to get the party going.

He'd put on his headphones and seamlessly changed the music to lo-fi hip hop.

"Wanna get some fresh air?" asked Mark.

I nodded, hypnotized by Mark's smiling face so close to mine.

We came out of the house and trailed into a garden in the backyard. There was a gazebo that was naturally decorated by growing vines and flowers. It was a private and quiet space away from the party going on inside the house. We sat down on the bench as we talked and sipped on our drinks.

"How do you like the party so far?" Mark asked, breaking the silence.

"So far, so good. Thanks for taking me here. You barely know me."

"If there's a party to meet total strangers, this is it."

My phone beeped and I wondered who would have texted me at this time.

"Sorry, I just have to check my phone really quick" as I grabbed my phone from my bag. I got a text message from Laura. She was asking if I wanted to have brunch on Saturday. I said yes. *I love having brunch with Laura. I can't wait to tell her about Mark.*

"Your boyfriend checking in on you?" Mark asked half-jokingly.

"Huh – No, it's not. I mean, it's my best friend." I laughed awkwardly.

Why is he asking about boyfriend stuff? Is he even remotely interested in me? Me and him? Is he drunk? No, Emma – you're delusional. It's just a simple question. It doesn't mean that this deliciously hot handsome devil wants to know if you have a boyfriend.

"So, you DON'T have a boyfriend?" Mark asked as he sat closer and turned to me.

Okay, he does want to know – but why? Does he want to set me up with someone he knows would be interested, or just curious about my personal affairs?

"Uhm, no I don't have a boyfriend. Do you?" I responded back.

"Do I have a boyfriend? No. No, I don't." We both laughed.

"How about a girlfriend?" I pried, right away regretting my question.

"Not yet." He smiled, and winked at me accompanied by a sharp clicking sound he made from the side of his mouth.

Oh my God. I think I'm gonna have an aneurism. What does he mean "not yet"? Is it "not YET" — meaning maybe in the future with me? I think I'm overthinking all of this. But how could I not? Here we are under this beautiful gazebo, in the heart of a lovely garden under the stars, it all seemed so... deeply romantic. How come there's only two of us here? I need some clarification.

"Sorry, what do you mean by 'not yet'? Is there a girl you're currently pursuing... that might... be your girlfriend in the future?" I pried even more.

"Yeah, you could say that. I really like this one." Mark replied as he looked up thoughtfully at the sky.

"Oh, I see." my heart sank with the thought of him wanting another girl.

"I'm just not sure if she's interested in me." He slowly looked back at me as if waiting for my response.

"How could she not? Dude, do you know how... cute you are?"

"So, you think I'm cute?" Mark blushed like a six-year-old boy confessing his love to his first-grade crush.

"Okay, let's change the subject now, bro."

What the... why the heck did I call him bro.

"Alright fair enough, three rapid fire question and answer... Ready?" Mark looked like he was taking this game seriously.

"Ok, Go!" I said without any idea of how this works.

"Favorite movie?"

"Casablanca."

"Favorite food?"

"Chinese."

"Favorite flower?"

"Pink peonies."

"Alright, you did good! Those were pretty fast answers." Mark laughed.

A few hours later, we saw Jay walking towards us.

"You guys want more beer?" Jay called out.

Mark looked at his watch "Damn, it's three-thirty in the morning! I better take you home now, Emma, you must be tired" Mark said to me; I hadn't even realized we were there for that long.

As we stood up, I realized that I didn't want to go home yet if I could instead spend more time with Mark, but I guess good things come to an end.

"Time went by so fast. I didn't realize it's three-thirty in the morning."

"Neither did I," said Mark.

"If you're too tired to drive, you guys could sleep in the guest rooms." Jay offered.

"No man, thanks but I'm good to drive."

As Mark drove me home, I felt as if I wanted nothing else but to stay in his car for as long as possible. At this hour, the drive to my apartment went by very fast. *Damn it, why are there no vehicles around at three in the morning?* I cursed to myself.

Mark stopped and parked his car in front of my apartment. I collected my bag and got ready to open the passenger door.

"Hold up, before you go, let me read your palm." Mark said as he turned to me and gently took my right hand, turning it facing up. "I'm kind of a psychic, you know."

"Alright then, how much do you charge?" I grinned back at him.

"First one's always free." He smiled and winked at me again with that impressive click sound.

While holding my hand, he slowly traced the lines on my palm with his index finger. I felt this tremendous need inside me to be near him, and as if reading my mind, he started getting closer and closer to me. Only a few inches apart and he could press his lips against mine. I stared at his lips as I bit my lower lip, full of desire. Taking a deep breath, I was intoxicated with the power of his masculine scent.

"So, tell me about my future..." I mumbled as I pulled away a little.

"I see you going on another date... with this guy who really likes you." he replied scrutinizing my palm.

"Uh Huh... And why is that?"

"Because he can't stop thinking about you."

His eyes locked with mine; every inch of my body was electrified by his caressing eyes as if penetrating my soul. I couldn't help but felt weak in my knees, unable to utter a single word for minutes.

"Hmm, we shall see... if your palm reading is accurate." I finally said as I blushed. I collected my bag and exited the car.

"Good night, Emma. I had an awesome time with you."

"Me as well!" I called back as I waved goodbye.

"Jay's going to have another party next month, I hope you'll come with me again! He said you're kinda cool."

Really? They were talking about me, and Jay thinks I'm cool! He did make a really good mojito.

"Sounds good, thanks Jay!" *Oh fuck! What the hell did I just say! His name is Mark! Mark! Mark! The handsome Mark who picked me up, brought me to the party and dropped me home. Why did I say Jay?!*

"Oh, I mean Mark! I'm so sorry... must be the mojitos!" I waved it off, laughing nervously.

"Uh, no worries... he does make some pretty bomb drinks," mumbled Mark.

"I'm so sorry! I'm just tired... Uhm... have a good night!" I turned around and hurried up to my apartment front door not looking back. I embarrassed myself by calling my date by his best friend's name!

CHAPTER THREE

Blood Moon

Normally my Fridays consisted of me being alone in my basement-level studio apartment, downing cheap three-liter boxes of wine, and watching *He's Just Not That Into You*. This Friday was phenomenal. I went to a cool house party with my handsome date. Mark and I had made a connection, things were happening, and everything was great until the moment I had to ruin it with a brain fart.

I woke up to Laura's phone call the next morning reminding me of our brunch date at a gorgeous lakeside café called Blue Lagoon. I ordered a big plate of frittata and a cup of coffee while Laura had a bagel with cream cheese and a pumpkin spice latte. She was wearing a formal sleeveless black sheath dress paired with black kitten heels, as if she was just invited for a tea with the Queen. I was wearing a grey hoodie with *Dickies* logo on my chest, black stretch yoga pants and a pair of white sneakers.

"Is there a funeral?" I asked Laura with a smirk on my face.

"Gym slut!" Laura retorted. Yeah, she hit the nail right on the head.

"Joke's on you, I don't exercise!" *Oh good, I proudly announced that I'm a lazy slut.*

"I've missed you!"

"Well, what can I say?" I fake blushed and quickly fired back "You look gorgeous! I'm sensing *a Breakfast at Tiffany's* look?"

"Oh My God! I knew you would get it!" Laura laughed.

I told her about my wonderful date with the most handsome guy I'd ever met. I described Mark to Laura like he's Captain America, and that we ended the night with this steamy, flirtatious gaze at each other. But then it all ended with a disaster because of my stupid brain-mouth coordination.

"Good!" said Laura.

"What do you mean, *Good*? I fucked up!"

"So, he won't believe that you're obsessed with him!"

"I'm not obsessed with him!"

"Then why are we still here talking about this guy for two hours?"

"You're right... I just... I wish I didn't..."

"It's one date. You barely know him. If he really likes you, he will ask you out again."

Hearing that made me feel better. Laura had always been my voice of reason. She always gave me the hard truth. We've been best friends forever and I couldn't imagine my life without her.

Mark arrived late for our Monday class. He sat right in the front row; I only saw the back of his head from afar. There was no group discussion that day, so I couldn't even use that as an excuse to be close to him. I wished he'd talk to me again. I spent all weekend thinking about every moment we shared. His smile, his eyes, his scent... the moment we almost kissed. Those were some of the moments I wished a time machine really existed so I could go back and relive them.

After the class ended, I walked out of the classroom at a glacial pace. I was not in the mood to do anything that day. I just wanted to go home, binge-watch Game of Thrones, and stuff my face with a tub full of fried chicken.

"Hey Emma, what's your next class? A familiar voice said behind me.

"Mark!... Oh, hi! In half an hour..."

"Cool, want to get a cup of coffee?"

"Sure, yeah, I need one so bad... Oh and I've got to get my chocolate fix!" I yelled as if I abruptly got jacked up on Red Bull.

Mark and I walked over to the University cafeteria. We both got an Americano for coffee and sat at one of the tables right in the main hall. It was so busy, filled with loud murmurs and chatters of everyone passing by. I excused myself and rushed off to the vending machine nearby.

A guy wearing a brown leather jacket and dark denim jeans was standing by the vending machine pondering the selections. He turned back and smiled at me. I smiled back to this handsome *James Dean --*

Oh. My. God. It's the guy who gave his change for my chocolate bar!

"Out of change?" he asked, a smile on his face.

"No – I'm good, thanks."

"Sorry about getting you the wrong chocolate bar last time."

"No worries, you've been so kind to me. Let me get you something this time!"

"No need to..."

"Please... I felt so bad running away last time – I was just so late for class." I stammered as I started pulling out a handful of quarters.

"No, it was my fault. I was just standing by, but my mind was somewhere else."

"Oh, that happens to all of us."

"I'm Jason by the way." He smiled at me and reached out his hand.

"Emma..." I shook his hand and started shoving quarters into the machine. "So, what's your poison?"

"Well, Mr. Big..." Jason let out a chuckle.

As I laughed, I noticed he seemed a little embarrassed. He's a bit shy, though he looked like a bad-boy leading man with the outfit he had on. This time he wasn't wearing his eyeglasses and looked so different, so... attractive. I finished putting the exact change into the vending machine and handed the Mr. Big bar to Jason.

"So, I guess I'll see you again in our next chocolate run."

"I'll make sure to be here." Jason smiled and watched me walk back to my table with Mark.

"Flirting with Mr. Big?" Mark teased me as I sat down and sipped my coffee.

"What, no! Just... returning a favor."

"So, where's my chocolate?" Mark smirked at me.

"Oh... but I didn't know what you wanted..."

"I'm just joking," Mark gently brushed a lock of my hair behind my left ear. "Emma, about last Friday... I had an amazing time with you.".

Oh, thank God. So, I didn't totally blow it. I could still save this potential love affair once and for all.

"Uhm... so, about my palm reading... do you think it will happen soon?" I glanced up from my coffee.

Mark's face brightened like a sky beaming with a rainbow after the rain.

"I'd like to take you out to my favorite restaurant tonight. Would you like to go on a date with me?"

"I'd love to." I smiled back. Suddenly everything seemed so right.

Andy and I had been spending a lot of time lately. He turned out to be one of the friendliest and funniest people I'd ever known. I had a feeling that Andy was one of those rich kids who just bought whatever they wanted only because they could. Andy had been itching to go shopping all day so after our last class in the afternoon, we sped over to his favorite department store, Holt Renfrew. He drove his brand-new Range Rover to the place like an ambulance driver.

"Andy! Drive fast enough? I don't really plan on dying today!" I said nervously.

"Well, my dear, in the unlikely event that you do perish as the result of my efficient driving, what type of casket would you prefer I order for you – wood veneer or laminate?"

"Laminate? Andy, are you cheaping out on me!? You better bury my ass in a bronze or copper casket – I heard they're resistant to rust and corrosion!"

"It saddens me that you know that - but done. Veneer it is!" Andy said with a short laugh.

"What would I do without friends like you?" I said while miming a blissful look. We both laughed as we walked through the door. Inside the store was immaculate and stunning. The place even smelled *rich*.

Andy had been dying to get something from Alexander McQueen. Not even within two minutes, he saw a cotton short-sleeve shirt with various insects printed on it, and to my disbelief, he was seriously considering it!

Now, I really liked Andy. I also wanted to be a supportive friend, but this shirt made him look like he's got some awful bug infestation problem. The design was my main concern until I happened to glance down at the price tag. It read "$1,000.00". My eyes literally bulged out of my sockets.

Uhm, whoever's in-charge in the price-tagging department must either be high or drunk. Or both I suppose.

"This... can't be right." I told Andy as I held up the tag.

"What's not right?"

"A thousand dollars for a cotton shirt?" I cried incredulously.

"Oh, you're right, there must be some mistake." Andy shook his head as he went over the shirt "This is limited edition, so I was expecting it to be *way* more! Oh! And it's the last one! I MUST get it!" He looked back at me flashing his brilliant grin.

"What the... Is that a cockroach, a beetle, a dragonfly, and a maggot...?" as I point to each bug design print on the shirt.

Andy looked at me, "Emma, don't be so uncultured, it's *Art*. I'm collecting McQueen art."

"You know your bug shirt costs more than my monthly rent, right?"

"Mmm kay, well I think that says much more about your current living situation than it does my shirt." Andy said with a wink as I shook my head and laughed.

As I continued to browse, I walked over to the fanny-pack isle noticing that each item costs twelve hundred dollars minimum.

"Andy, do you want to sleep on it tonight? Maybe see if you still want it tomorrow?" I said as i turned around, realizing that he wasn't there anymore. "Uh, Andy?"

"Huh? What are you talking about? I already bought it. It was only a grand." He said as nonchalantly as I would say fifty cents.

"Now, let's get some gelato. My treat!" He pulled me with him as we left the store – sorry, boutique as Andy would say. We walked down the road to the nearest gelato shop and ordered our favorites, chocolate for me and pistachio for him.

"You know — I imagine you'd be killing it in Fashion Institute of Technology or something like that... Why don't you apply?" I pried as I devoured my gelato.

"Yeah, I guess... but I'm supposed to be the rightful heir to my family's cat food empire."

"Right — I shall call you *Catnip King* one day!" I laughed, impressed with my quick comeback.

"More like *Queen of the Catnip*!" Andy laughed as he mocked a pose.

"Too bad... I would've loved to wear your maggot print cardigan from your debut Collection assuming you'll give it to me for free."

"Oh, sweetie. Of course, it's not for free." Andy grinned at me as if picturing himself walking on the runway after a successful launch of his Maggot collection.

We spent the entire afternoon talking over coffee. Things got serious as he confessed to me that he had not yet come out to his parents, afraid that they would disown him.

"How could they not know? I mean, you don't exactly hide it..."

"I don't say much when I see them. I'm different with them, I suppose."

"They haven't noticed at all?"

"No. They're very religious — if they knew, they'd shun me."

"Shun you? What is this, the Village? Isn't it hard hiding who you are?"

"Yeah, it kills me..." He slumped back into his chair. "I mean... I don't want to be a CEO of a cat food company. I want to be the next Alexander McQueen!"

Yes, Andy was spoiled but that came with the price of pretending to be someone he wasn't. Maybe he lavishly spent his parents' money as some sort of subconscious revenge for a lifetime of not being able to be himself. I really liked Andy, and as much I wanted to criticize some of his behavior, I understood why.

It seemed Andy and I had the opposite life situation. His parents had a lot of money and had provided generously to support his luxurious lifestyle since birth. He'd been handed success on a silver platter yet what he truly wanted was to just be himself and pursue his own dreams. I wished I had Andy's life not because of the wealth but because he had a family.

My early childhood wasn't so fortunate. My mother had me when she was not ready to have a child. From what I knew, she resented me for wrecking her future plans as I was the result of one night of passion with a stranger. She saw me as a mistake from the start. My father also didn't want to have anything to do with me. They didn't love each other, and they certainly didn't love me. My mother abandoned me when I was only a few months old. She had made the decision to start a new life in another city not wanting to be a part of my life. My grandparents raised me instead and gave me a home. I grew up not having any taste of luxury, with just enough to get by. I always wondered what it would feel like to have parents growing up. But I knew I was also lucky enough that my grandparents loved me, and they were all I had.

My grandfather and I were out fishing by the side of the river one day when all of a sudden, he fell down onto his back and clutched his chest as if he couldn't breathe. Just like that, he was gone. I was only 8 years old at the time. Then, twelve years later, my grandmother rested on her final sleep and did not wake up. It felt as though I had no one, no real family.

I wished that one day, my mom and dad would be a part of my life somehow. I knew that they didn't think about me... But I thought about them a lot. I wished nothing else but to see them and hug them. Maybe one day they'd be back to say they were sorry and that they loved me.

I was excited to see Mark for our date that night. He said he'd take me out to his favorite restaurant. *I wonder what I should wear. If Mark's taking me to his favorite restaurant, it might be fancy.*

I didn't want to assume anything, but I'd rather be over-dressed than underdressed for a special date. I had a red A-line wrap dress sitting in my closet that I had not worn since I bought it. I'd never had a special occasion to wear it until now! I paired this dress with black leather pumps, completing the look with faux gold earrings.

Only a few moments after I had finished getting ready, I received a text message from Mark.

'I'm outside your apartment. I'll wait until you're ready.'

'I'm ready. I'll be right out.' I messaged back.

I came out of the front entrance of my apartment feeling like I'm about to head off to some fancy charity gala. I walked to Mark's car and opened his passenger door. He was looking at me like he picked up the wrong person from a different address.

Oh no! Did I do it too much?

I smiled at Mark as I fastened my seatbelt. He looked dashing in his semi-casual grey jacket and dark denim jeans. His scent was intoxicating. I just wanted to bury my face against his chest and leave a trail of kisses on the side of his neck.

"You look beautiful. Love that dress on you."

"Thanks." I smiled as I looked away, trying not to show how pleased I was that a couple of hours of preparation was worth it.

"I found the best Chinese restaurant in the city, it's pretty close to here. You said you love Chinese food, right?"

"Definitely, I do! I'm excited to check it out!"

I'm so relieved that we're going for Chinese food. I'm starving, and I've been craving Asian food all week.

We drove for about five minutes without saying much. He parked on the street just outside of a small strip mall and we walked towards a restaurant called "Red Dragon". It's in between a small Korean grocery store and a Laundromat. As we walked inside, there was a long hallway with low dim lights illuminating from the wall lamps. The ceiling was high, and the walls were made out of brown walnut wood. A red carpet covered the hallway floor leading to the hostess station.

The place looks like the headquarters for the triad in Rush Hour 2. I thought, looking around.

A very friendly lady welcomed us and led us to our table. As we walked into the main dining hall, I was absolutely blown away by how beautiful it was inside, night and day based on the outside entrance. It was so elegant! There was an elevated balcony inside where there were more upholstered booth seats, marble floors, and chandeliers. No one was there but Mark and me. It seemed so grand for such a very private and unknown place. All of a sudden, we heard subtle classical piano music playing in the background from the speakers hidden in the ceilings. I must admit, I was pleasantly surprised. It was very romantic.

"It's really nice here, Mark. So how many girls have you brought here before me?"

"Dozens, I've lost count really," Mark smirked at me as I rolled my eyes. "Honestly, you're the only one, Emma."

"So, you say!" I teased Mark as I admire the unexpected grandeur of the place.

We ordered barbecue chicken, spicy beef satay, deluxe fried rice, and seafood Chow Mein. The server carefully walked toward us carrying a tray of aromatic and steaming hot, freshly cooked dishes. We looked at each other in disbelief at how amazing the food tasted as we sampled them one by one.

Mark and I talked about what was going on in school, our favorite movies, music, and television shows. It was so easy to talk with Mark. It's as if time stopped when we were together. He laughed at my silly jokes, and I couldn't help but do the same with him. I wanted to know more about him. I found myself becoming more and more interested in his thoughts and dreams in life. He made me feel like he truly cared about who I was.

After supper, Mark and I drove aimlessly around the city. I didn't care where we went. I rolled down the passenger window slightly for some fresh air and saw the most beautiful night sky.

"Wow! Mark, look at the moon!" I marveled at the red-orange full moon that appeared to be much bigger and closer to the horizon than I'd ever seen before. It gleamed so near that it felt as though I could almost reach out and touch it, pluck it right out from its starry field.

"Oh, that's a "blood moon", it only appears when there's a total lunar eclipse. I know the perfect place where we'll get the best view." Mark winked at me.

We drove all the way to a little town called Newport for about half an hour outside the city. Mark stopped at the town's small liquor store to get a couple of beers before it closed. He parked the car by the side of the road close to where the water from the river joins the dam. The rush of water flowing down from the river surrounded us with a peaceful ambience. No one else was there at that hour but us. There were bright tall lamp posts around the floodgate that made me feel safe even though we were alone. The full moon's reflection illuminated against the darkness of the water with white pelicans congregating nearby.

"I love it when the moon seems so much bigger, you feel like you can go there someday." I said wistfully while staring up at the night sky.

We both sat down on the grass near the river, taking everything in as he opened two beers and handed me mine. We clinked our bottles together in a silent toast before taking a sip.

"So, tell me," Mark turned to me, breaking the silence. "What's one thing that's missing in your life right now?" He looked at me and quietly waited for my answer though I must admit the depth of the question caught me off-guard. I had to think hard about what was missing in my life, and I knew for a fact that there was a lot. I looked back up at the moon as if it held all the answers I needed for this existential question and sighed deeply.

"It's hard to find what's missing when you're happy with what you have," I finally answered back. Truth be told this was exactly what I was thinking. I couldn't ask for anything more from the universe when I was right next to a person that filled my heart.

"You always surprise me, Emma. I wish I would have met you a lot sooner." Mark's brown eyes glimmered as the moon shone on his face.

Mark and I stared at the full blood-orange moon. There was a peaceful silence between us with only a few echoes of the water flowing and the birds roving in the dark sky.

"I like you, Emma. I like you so much... I'm happy when I'm with you. I... can't stop thinking about you."

"I... like you too Mark... So much..."

Mark lifted my chin as I looked up to meet his mesmerizing eyes. He gently ran his hands down my face, cupping the sides of my jaw, inching his head closer and closer for his lips to meet mine. I felt electricity running down my spine and butterflies in my stomach. I closed my eyes eager to receive his kiss. His smooth, juicy lower lip pushed gently against mine. I felt a sudden rush inside me while lightly running my hands at the nape of his neck, across his shoulders and down his back. We kissed passionately all through the night with only the peering blood moon as our witness.

CHAPTER FOUR

Passion in the Lake House

Mark and I had been inseparable ever since the night we spent under the blood-orange full moon. We spent time in between classes together to have lunch or coffee, stroll around campus, or walk in the nearby park. He told me that autumn was his favorite season because of all the beautiful colors with the leaves turning amber and crimson, the cool fall breeze, Halloween and Thanksgiving, hot cocoa, flannel shirts, and pumpkin spice lattes.

We were old souls. We both loved collecting vinyl records from older eras. I personally loved music from the 1930's to 1960's – Billie Holiday, Ella Fitzgerald, Edith Piaf, Frank Sinatra, Dean Martin. Mark loved old movies from that era – Citizen Kane, Casablanca, Gone with the Wind, Rebel Without a Cause, Rear Window. We'd go on dates perusing little shops that sell vintage clothing, old books, and antique knick-knacks. I had a deep appreciation of things that seemed to have been handed down through multiple generations – old suitcases, French Provincial dressers, mid-century credenzas, 18th century oil lamps and manual typewriters. My apartment was filled with these old items from the past – it gave me a sense of identity as if I lived in another decade. Mark and I hung out in my apartment to watch old classic movies that perpetuated the golden age of cinema. He loved to cook, and he was darn good at it. I was amazed at how well he worked in the kitchen with such grace and confidence.

The more time the two of us spent together, the more we got to know each other. Little things like how he hated green peas, mussels, and blue cheese — how he used to play the piano and competed in track and field when he was in high school, and that he made short videos and posted them on YouTube. He wanted to become a filmmaker in Hollywood someday. He downplayed his skills in making films, but I had seen his work and instantly knew he had a good eye for cinematography. I admired him for pursuing what he loved. I felt like I'd known him for years even though we'd only been together for a short period of time.

One of the things Mark loved to do was to go on hikes, so one warm afternoon we went to a place called Cedar Falls where he took me hiking. It was a lush forest covered with fir and cedar trees. Fallen tree trunks and stumps alongside the trail blended in with the lush moss that thrived in the moist soil below. The trail led us towards the sound of rushing water from the falls dropping a couple hundred feet below. The cascade of water was intimidating and yet somehow serene. The view at the top of the falls was mesmerizing as if fairies and elves lived underneath protecting its beauty and abundance. I've never felt such peacefulness and contentment before. It's as if I've been living in a cave wasting my life not discovering the beauty I had been so ignorant to see.

"This is beautiful... I can't believe I've never done this before." I finally said while staring out at the fall foliage.

"You've never gone hiking before?"

"I've lived strictly within the city's forty-mile radius."

"So, you've never gone camping, canoeing, white-water rafting...."

"No. No. And oddly yes, if you count the time I tumbled over into a deep pothole while walking to school."

"Well, that must have been one fierce pothole! Okay... why don't you and I do something a little more mellow, like spending a weekend together at a cabin?" Mark winked and flashed me with a flirty smile.

"Hmmm. Who else will be there?"

"No one else – you will have me all to yourself."

"Will there be s'mores and hot chocolate?"

"It would be a crime for there not to be" Mark gazed into my eyes and slowly lifted my chin. His lips softly touched mine. He transported me to another world whenever we kissed as if I was floating on cloud nine. Every day I felt myself falling in love with Mark. I wished he felt the same for me. I've never been so happy, so free. In the middle of the forest with all its glory, I felt like the luckiest girl in the world. I didn't need anything else but Mark. I was perfectly content and at peace, just being with him, wherever that may be.

The strong splashing of water from the falls and the ambient breeze swaying a cluster of leaves was the perfect music to our tryst. I slowly pulled away from his kiss and gently opened my eyes. I smiled at him not hiding my satisfaction from what just happened.

"So, whose cabin is it, anyway? Is it far from the city?"

"It's my parents' cabin, about two hours north outside the city. Would you be free next weekend?"

"I'm gonna have to check with my other boyfriend." I teased Mark.

"Andy? He's busy, I had asked him first, but he said he couldn't make it. So here we are." Mark laughed as he stood up with me.

"I really don't think you're his type. So you're stuck with me." I grinned as I wrapped my arms around Mark's waist.

"That's true, he's out of my league, really." Mark and I continued kissing as if it's the last time we were ever going to be together. After our lovely walk, we drove home talking endlessly about our plans for our cabin getaway next weekend.

It was a sunny Saturday morning with a beguiling autumn chill in the air. Mark picked me up from my apartment at exactly ten o'clock. I packed two day's change of clothes for our romantic cabin getaway. As Mark drove the car on the highway, I rolled down the passenger window and leaned my head over to feel the rush of wind against my face. Mark played an array of 90's alternative rock classics from The Smashing Pumpkins, Green Day and Nirvana. My job as a shotgun driver was to make sure I offered snacks every fifteen minutes and be a jester/lip-sync performer at the same time.

We arrived at his parents' cabin by the lake at noon. It was a welcoming humble cabin, ideally found on a small plot of land with a million-dollar view. I couldn't contain my excitement when I saw the cabin's dock leading out into the lake. The water seemed deep enough to dive in. It was tempting to just run and jump into the crystal-clear water but it was unbearably cold to swim at that time of the year. There was a canoe right outside the house by the steel patio swing. Towering pine trees provided intimate privacy surrounding the cabin. As we went inside, I noticed the interior of the cabin was painted with the same crisp, white paint as the outside. It gave a feeling of hominess to its coastal-inspired interior design. There was an airy porch enclosed with wide bright windows, and intimate wicker chairs in the entry. In the living room, there was a comfy beige plush sofa stacked with powder-blue pillows and rattan chairs. On the ceiling was a spiral bohemian shell chandelier. The walls were meticulously adorned with colorful seascape paintings. There was a sunny breakfast nook underscored by a braided rug and deliberately mismatched chairs. The rustic exposed wood beams and hardwood floors contrasted beautifully with the bright white paint on the walls, doors, and furniture.

There were only two bedrooms in the house. Mark showed me the first bedroom, which had a wrought iron queen bed with white linens and pillows overlooking the lake. There's a sea-blue hand-woven rug on the floor, an antique wooden nightstand, and a brass vintage Edison-bulb lamp. The second bedroom had exactly the same decoration but this one had a king size bed and a huge portrait of Mark's parents on the wall.

Mark and I brought some hotdogs and buns, s'mores, chips, fresh cut-up fruit, cheese and salami, a six-pack of beer and two bottles of wine – a Chardonnay and a Merlot. A full feast for a weekend at the Cabin! Later in the afternoon, we decided to paddle the canoe out onto the lake with a couple of beers and some snacks. The water was calm, and the sky was clear, the wind was forgiving and nobody else from the neighboring cabins was in the water.

"This is really nice, the cabin looks so small from this distance." I said looking back at the shoreline.

"Well, it is small… we're not *that* far from the shore." Mark smiled as he paddled.

"I love your parents' cabin, it's so cozy and relaxing — it's perfect!" I stated, declaring my appreciation with animated gestures that almost tipped the canoe.

"I'm glad you love it babe, but try not to tip the boat over or we'll have to swim to shore, possibly getting hypothermia." He calmly reached for my hand as he planted a kiss on my cheek.

"Uhm, what did you call me?"

"You heard me…" Mark blushed.

"Yes, sugar plum." I teased, wiggling the boat while he paddled.

"Babe!" Mark yelled in the middle of the lake.

Mark and I went back to the cabin just before sunset. He gathered some wood and started a fire on the firepit. We roasted hotdogs and s'mores. We had been paddling the canoe on the lake all afternoon. Needless to say, we were famished and tired. Those hotdogs tasted like the best meal we'd ever had. Mark took a couple of wine glasses from the cabin and popped open a bottle of Chardonnay. It was refreshingly cold and delicious. He then played some romantic jazz music from his phone and covered me with a cozy white blanket. We sat on the metal swing near the fire and clinked our glasses together watching the sunset cascade. The view was sublime with pink and orange hues deep on the horizon. As twilight fell upon us, the fire provided sufficient light and warmth to push back the darkness. The water was so near that we could hear an endless batch of waves breaking against the shore. He made sure that there was enough wood near the pit to burn throughout the night. The moon and the stars gleamed brightly against the cloudless pitch-black sky.

" *'She walks in beauty, like the night'* " Mark whispered looking at me " *'Of cloudless climes and starry skies; And all that's best of dark and bright, meet in her aspect and her eyes'*... I couldn't help myself, the way you look against this starry night just reminded me of those lines from Byron..." Mark said trailing off.

"That's beautiful."

"Oh, we finished the whole bottle of Chardonnay." Mark said as he held the wine bottle upside down as proof.

"Should we open another one?" I asked while I took the bottle from Mark.

"Are you trying to get me drunk? Mark smiled and winked at me

"Is that what it takes for you to say you love me?" I teased but right away regretted it.

Mark gazed at me; I saw the burning fire reflecting in his eyes.

"I don't need alcohol to say it. I'm not even close to getting drunk... You don't know how much you mean to me, Emma. I've never felt so close to anyone as when I'm with you. I find myself thinking about you when we're not together. I'm happy when I see you happy. I feel the need to protect you. I'd do anything for you. Emma, I love you."

I froze with his words. I can't believe I was hearing all of these from the person I was truly in love with. I looked into his eyes with disbelief and a knot in my stomach.

"I love you too, Mark... I've never loved anyone like this before. You're everything I ever wanted..."

Mark hugged me tight, and I gripped him tighter with overflowing joy, not wanting to let go. He stared into my eyes and raced to kiss me. This time, our kiss was more passionate than it had ever been before. My hands caressed his broad shoulders and tight arms as he held onto my waist; his hand was slowly sliding up under my shirt. I didn't stop him. I wanted him now more than ever. In the darkness of the night, the fire died faster than it should have. Mark's hand slid up my back and seamlessly unhooked my bra. I was filled with anticipation as he lifted my shirt and gently placed one hand on my breast while the other gripped my back. I held onto Mark's head surrendering myself to him. He gradually planted gentle kisses on my bosom.

I moaned with lust as I felt a suction force titillating the center of each side of my chest.

"Oh Mark..." I murmured.

Mark carried me inside the cabin, locked the front door, and led me to the cozy bedroom. He laid me down in bed gently as he kissed my lips, then my neck. I pulled up his shirt and exposed his firm and toned stomach. Taking a deep breath, I tried to contain my carnal urges for this gorgeous man. I kissed Mark's chest working my way down to his stomach. I couldn't resist it, I knew it was weird, but I did it anyway – I licked his abs and traced my fingers through the crevices of his torso.

By this time, I've unleashed my inner slut like a phoenix rising from the ashes. I unzipped Mark's jeans and proceeded to pull them down, hearing no protest from him.

Mark kissed my breasts once again, on each side, slowly planting kisses down my stomach. Going down to my navel and finally stopping in between my legs. I moaned softly as he kissed me passionately where he had never kissed me before. I looked down at Mark pleading with him to not stop until finally, waves of pleasure struck me as I rolled my eyes back and gripped onto the headboard. My body was rising in ecstasy. I moaned loudly and shouted out Mark's name as the rushing flow of orgasm momentarily paralyzed me. I looked back down at Mark with eyes that said *'Thank You, Sex God'*. He seemed pleased with his work like some fine artist who just finished his masterpiece. I felt compelled to show Mark what I had up my sleeve. I flipped our positions and kissed his torso one more time; then down his stomach, stopping at where I could tell he was desiring. *Mmm, I love a good Popsicle during a hot summer day*. Mark moaned in satisfaction but stopped me before he could lose control.

I hopped on top of Mark like I was off to some bold adventure. We both moaned as I slowly lowered myself on his manhood and felt the unwavering sensation of him being inside me. I rode him like a beautiful Arabian horse in the Sahara Desert. Our hearts were beating fast as we both reached our peak at the same time. Feeling the rush of him exploding inside me brought me to another intense orgasm; I didn't want it to stop. Inaudible groaning and moaning followed after we exhausted all our energy for the night.

"I love you babe..." Mark whispered in my ear.

"I love you too..." I placed my arms on his chest and my head on his shoulder and fell blissfully asleep.

CHAPTER FIVE

First Fight

Mark felt like my soul mate, like we found each other after centuries of searching. I wanted to share everything with him. Maybe it was an obsession... Maybe it was only because I had longed for someone to trust. I adored him like the sun. He gave me a reason to feel alive. I believed that he loved me as much as I loved him. For me, that was enough. My life had just begun.

One evening, Mark and I met with Laura at a quaint little Italian restaurant that served the best gourmet pizza I'd ever had. The bacon double cheeseburger pizza was adorned with crispy strip-bacon, lean ground beef, sumptuous cheddar and mozzarella cheese, drizzled with mouth-watering homemade BBQ Sauce.

"Where'd you find this place, Mark?" Laura asked, seemingly impressed.

"We played a gig here about a year ago."

"Oh, so you're in a band? What do you play?"

"Guitar... It was a friend's wedding. We played as a present to the bride and groom."

"Are you telling me, I'm dating a future rock star, and I didn't even know it?" I teased Mark as he blushed.

"One can only dream, babe." He mumbled. Then he suddenly got excited, "We're having a fundraising event for my cousin this weekend at Jack's Café. You guys should come!"

"Of course, babe, what's the fundraiser for?" I asked while holding Mark's hand.

"My fifteen year-old cousin, Melissa, has leukemia. We thought that we'd gather friends to help out with her medical bills."

"I'd love to come. Laura, you're coming too, right?" I faced Laura who was already nodding her head in affirmation.

"Awesome! There'll be raffle draws for donated prizes but we've yet to find a singer as part of the entertainment." Mark said, seemingly worried.

"Wow, seems legit. Just let me know how I could help, okay?" I leaned over and kissed Mark. Laura gave us this disgusted look.

"You guys — get a room!" Laura said as she demonstrated a fake gagging motion as I excused myself to go to the restroom.

When I walked back to our table, I saw Laura showing Mark her phone. She suddenly pulled it away when she saw me coming back to my seat. I gave them both a *what's-going-on-here* look as they both stared at me in silence.

"Who died, and am I invited to the funeral?" I said jokingly but felt really disgusted at my distasteful punch line.

"About how you could help with the fundraising event —" Laura trailed off.

"Yeah, of course! What can I do?" I looked over at Mark while he gave me a bemused look.

"Well, Babe, is this really you?" Mark asked as he showed me Laura's phone, which was playing a YouTube video.

Oh. My. God. It was my YouTube channel on the screen. I had six subscribers and a collection of three videos, each of which had at most fifteen views. The views were mainly from Laura and me watching my videos together. I created this account a few months back when Laura and I binge-watched *Netflix movies* with bags of Doritos and a couple bottles of homemade wine. We ended up pretty drunk in the end, and Laura convinced me to post videos of myself playing the ukulele and singing the old-timers' *Fly Me To The Moon, La Vie en Rose,* and *As Time Goes By.* This was supposed to be our own little secret, she promised to take this to her grave.

"You have a lovely unique voice. I've never heard anyone sing like that. You sound amazing!" Mark said looking at me astonished.

"You're only saying that because you're my boyfriend." I retorted back at Mark.

"Emma, your voice is both melancholic and soothing." Mark gazed at me.

"See, Emma... I told you so! Why do you think all my relatives are subscribed to you?" Lamented Laura as she took a sip of water.

"Because you forced them to." I murmured.

"You're a natural-born singer." Mark held my hands as he stared into my eyes.

"I was just telling Mark that you should perform at the café for the fundraising."

"What?! No, no, no... I can't." I strongly protested.

"But you're amazing, Emma. It would be a shame for you not to share your talent."

"I just can't... I'm sorry... I've never performed..." I said as I looked over to Laura.

"It's for my sick cousin Emma, please." Mark pleaded to me.

He was right, I did say I would do anything to help. I felt guilty about putting my own insecurities first so I agreed to sing. I practiced every night after I got home from school or work. I just needed to overcome my fear of messing up in front of an audience.

Saturday came and there were about a hundred people in the café. I wore a powder-blue turtleneck; light washed jeans and white sneakers. I put my hair up in a high ponytail with wisps of hair on the sides of my face. I was so nervous and terrified to go in the middle of the café where Mark had set up a makeshift stage for me. The café was decorated with warm, cozy string lights. The room was quite dim with one spotlight centered towards the chair where I was going to perform. I saw Laura sitting over in the corner with Andy and a few other friends.

Mark's cousin, Melissa, walked up to me. She had a frail figure and pale face. She looked at me with the warmest, affectionate smile as she opened her arms. I welcomed her.

Melissa gently spoke, "Thank you, Emma. I appreciate this so much. Mark showed me your YouTube videos and I was mesmerized by your voice. I'm now a big fan, and one of your subscribers! I'm so happy to see you today, and I can't wait to hear you sing live."

My heart melted with Melissa's words. Just like that, all my fears had vanished. I was going to perform for Melissa. She wanted to hear me sing! I took a deep breath and grabbed my ukulele waiting to go on stage ready to give it my all. As Mark called my name to come up, I looked for Melissa in the crowd and smiled at her. She gave me a big thumbs up, with a wide grin on her face. I smiled back and started singing.

□ 'Stars shining bright above you' □
'Night breezes seem to whisper "I love you"'
'Birds singing in the sycamore trees'
'Dream a little dream of me'□

I was carried away by the music and closed my eyes as the end of the song neared. When I was done, I slowly opened my eyes and saw Melissa shedding a tear while she applauded with the rest of the room. I saw smiling faces, loud applause, and words of appreciation from the crowd like "Oh hell yeah!", "Beautiful!", "Yas, girl!" – which I was ninety-nine per cent sure came from Andy. Everything went well. When I finished playing my last song and bid everyone goodbye, someone from the crowd yelled – "Just one more!" I felt flattered and elated that they liked my performance. But mainly, I was happy that Melissa had a wonderful fundraising event.

Mark came up to me afterwards and hugged me tight. "Thanks, Emma. You were wonderful. You made everyone's night. We couldn't have made this successful without you."

"Happy to help... I'm glad you liked it."

"They loved it, Emma! Everyone was taking photos and videos of your performance."

"Oh no... I hope they don't post them online!"

"Of course they'll post it online!"

Oh God, I was quite mortified about the idea of videos showing my full-face singing live somewhere out there in the inter-webs. I hoped it was all worth it.

A week later, Laura told me to go to Melissa's Fundraising Instagram page. She seemed eager for me to check it out. I was hoping to find out that Melissa was able to garner enough money for her medical bills. I was so happy that it was successful. I browsed down at the page and found a few videos of me singing from that night. I couldn't believe my eyes - over a million likes! The videos were being shared over and over to other people's Instagram accounts. *Am I famous?*

Before I could stop shaking my head, I heard the phone ring – it was Laura.

"Did you check out the Instagram page?" yelled Laura on the other line as I answered.

"Yes! Do you happen to have one million accounts?"

"Sweetie, I love you, you're my best friend. But I have no time for that!" giggled Laura.

"Well—how could it be? How did this happen?" I retorted, confused but excited.

"Mark made videos of you on YouTube and he also posted them on Instagram. You're going viral!"

"You're kidding!" I was quite embarrassed but thrilled at the same time.

I called Mark and he confessed to posting videos of me singing on the Internet. I couldn't believe he did that for me. He really believed in me.

"Maybe you'll consider posting more videos of yourself singing. People really love listening to you, babe. I can help film them too."

"I don't know... I mean, I only like to sing old songs..."

"Those songs complement your voice. I think you should sing the music that makes you feel happy."

It brought back memories of me and my grandma listening to music in our living room at night. I remembered singing along with Ella Fitzgerald and Billie Holiday records while my grandma knitted scarves. No one really taught me how to sing, I just learned by listening to the music that I loved. I sang because I loved entertaining my grandma but I was too afraid to show it to the world. For the first time in my life, I received validation from total strangers. Not that I needed it or ever felt the need to seek it, but it was just nice.

I was at the university cafeteria on a Tuesday afternoon waiting for Mark to meet me there while finishing up my assignments. My laptop was still making those weird noises and for the longest time I just ignored it as if it would self-diagnose and heal itself.

This was mainly for two reasons:

a.) Because I couldn't really afford to have it fixed if there was any major damage. And b.) Because I also couldn't afford to buy a new laptop in case my current rickety old laptop needed to retire and eventually rest in computer heaven.

Finally, I made an executive decision to back up my work in case I could not resuscitate it anymore. As I opened a new blank project, my laptop screen turned into a hazy rainbow color then... pitch black. It eventually just died even though it was fully charged.

"Oh My God.... No, no, no!!! Please....Mac Daddy!" I was teary-eyed holding the screen as I tried to revive my laptop back to life.

"What's wrong? Everything okay, Emma?" said a gentle worried voice near me.

I looked up, and there stood Jason right next to me. He looked so fresh and clean like a dreamy boy-next-door. I stared at him in amazement, almost making me forget my laptop woes.

I realized that I might have been a bit over dramatic with my reaction to my laptop's death.

"Hi Jason... No, my laptop... It's broken. It's old and I haven't fixed it, I knew something was wrong... but I didn't do anything... Now I've got nothing to use... I'm so stupid!" I trailed off frustrated and desperate.

"Don't be too harsh on yourself... Here, let me see..." Jason sat down across me and tinkered with my laptop doing some quick diagnostic. "You may just need a new SSD..."

Jason tried to explain every detail of what could be wrong with it but no matter how much I tried to understand my mind was a blank space. It was all gibberish to me — all I ever knew was how to turn it on, use programs, and then turn it off when I was done.

"You know, I can try to fix this for you..." Jason said sensing my dilemma. "I work at a computer repair shop and I have fixed hundreds of laptops before."

"Oh, that would be great but I just can't afford to have it fixed right now."

"Don't worry about it. I like fixing things. Computers, usually. Pro Bono for you."

"I couldn't — it's just too much to ask. I mean, this seems like a hard job... You barely know me."

"Don't be silly, Emma... You'd be doing me a favor since I like to tackle new projects, I'm awfully bored."

Jason saw the hesitation written all over my face as I gazed into his baby blue eyes.

"Okay... Would it make you feel better if I ask for a chocolate bar in return?" Jason grinned at me, as we locked eyes for a moment.

I smiled back at Jason although I still felt down. I really didn't have much option but to take a stranger's kindness. He said he could get it back to me in a week. I was just so grateful that he was helping me even though we hardly knew each other. I really needed my laptop for school.

"Are you sure? I don't want to bother you but I could really use the help."

"Of course, I promise."

"Oh you're my hero!" I yelled without thinking and hugged him out of the blue.

Jason was initially shocked, then he laughed when he saw my face turning red, as red as ripe beefsteak tomatoes.

"Oh, I'm so sorry..." I laughed nervously and looked down on the floor wanting to flee the scene of the crime.

"Don't be... I'll see you soon." Jason gazed at me one last time and walked away.

A couple minutes later, Mark came by and sat across me.

"So... I didn't know you meet your other boyfriends here too." Mark laughed but sounded a little fretful.

"Huh? What other boyfriends?" I forced a smile as I narrowed my eyes.

"Mr. Big — Did he give you another chocolate bar in exchange for a hug?"

"No, you're being ridiculous, babe! He's fixing my laptop because it's dead."

"Does he have a computer repair shop? That's his business, I guess?"

"He works at one, I couldn't afford to take it in but he's kind enough to fix my computer for free."

"Okay... and why would he do that?" Mark furrowed his brow as he looked at me.

"Because... he's fixed hundreds of computers before, and said he likes to fix things."

"Come on, you're smarter than that, Emma. Were you flirting with Mr. Big to get a free laptop repair?"

"Excuse me?"

"Did you offer him a chance for a date?"

"Mark, what the hell are you talking about? Don't be like that."

"Like what?"

"Like a total douchebag!" I said in a raging tone, way louder than I should have.

Mark got up from his chair and stormed away without looking back. I sat there staring at the table for twenty minutes wondering if I did something wrong to deserve his accusations. Regardless, the way he spoke to me cut deeply. I left thinking that we were both upset with each other but I thought we would patch things up in a few hours. He did not call or text me for the rest of the day.

Did we just have our first fight? What the heck just happened?

I tossed and turned in bed the next morning. I guess I felt guilty of Mark's accusation. Maybe he was right. Maybe he triggered something in me that made me say something mean. Maybe I was flirting with Jason. Maybe I shouldn't have locked eyes with Jason and hugged him — I didn't mean to. I wished I had reacted differently. I phoned Mark to apologize but he didn't answer. I fucked up and I needed to let him know how sorry I was.

CHAPTER SIX

Sexy Halloween Party

It was the night of our first fight, and I still hadn't heard from Mark. I was getting worried that he had not called me back and I had no idea where to find him. The longer those hours passed without him talking to me, the more I was convinced that he was really upset.

I saw Andy as I was walking out of the university.

"Why are you so glum, chum?" Andy asked, trying to bring me back to my consciousness.

"Oh, nothing..." I lied to Andy while staring blankly at the abyss.

"Hun, you look like you just lost all your money in some multi-level pyramid scheme!"

"Don't be silly," I let out a weak laugh. "Besides, I'm too broke to buy my way in."

"Shame. So, what's the problem? Did your crystal-healer cancel on you as well? Uhh! I swear, my life is in shambles. The unleashing of my Crown Chakra has been cancelled! Cancelled!"

"Rich people are weird." I said with a smirk on my face.

"So, is Mark taking you to a Halloween party?"

"We're fighting," I finally confessed. "We haven't spoken to each other since this morning."

"Oh sorry to hear that... does that mean he's available?!" Andy joked as he flipped his imaginary hair to the side.

"Honestly, you're the worst!" I blurted out. "Let's go to a party tonight!"

"Oh, okay... At last, the crazy comes out! Well, it just so happens that I heard of a Halloween party happening tonight! Maybe if I wear my slutty bunny costume, they'll let us in for free!" Andy laughed as he posed like a Playboy model with his hands above his head.

"Sure, and I'll pretend like I didn't see you slip twenty bucks to the bouncer."

"Twenty dollars? Ugh, Emma don't insult me, I would give the man at least a hundred... along with my number!" Andy winked at me.

"Always in good form Andy," I chuckled as we walked to the parking lot.

Later that evening Andy arrived at my apartment to pick me up and drive us to the Halloween party. For my costume, I barely made any effort. I was wearing all black. Black jeans, black sweater, black shoes, and a black witch hat. I didn't even put on any Halloween makeup. Andy, on the other hand, was not kidding when he said he was going all out. He came dressed in a skintight laced-up corset and skirt, fishnet stockings with garters hooked to the skirt, black shiny patent leather boots, and a long honey colored bombshell lock of hair. He looked way better than me. It was like standing right next to Angelina Jolie. And I'm not the least bit ashamed to admit it.

"Nice costume, you look like Tim Curry's understudy from the 'Rocky Horror Picture Show'." I jabbered.

"Jealous? Don't worry Emma, I'm not a homewrecker. I shan't steal Mark from you." Andy retorted with an air of sophistication and dignity.

"Not from a lack of trying I'd imagine? Though I must confess if someone were to steal him, it would be of some comfort to know it was you," I bantered.

"You and me both! Anyway, I see that you have really taken this costume party seriously! I mean all black with a witch hat, where do you find the time for such creativity?" Andy snickered.

"I thought I'd try something different!" I smirked. "Truthfully, I did want to get dressed up, but I couldn't stop thinking of Mark. He still hasn't called me back. What if he breaks things off with me? I mean, what if he's making out at this very moment? And with some slutty blonde hot bombshell? Andy, what should I do?" I said absolutely exasperated.

"I'm sure he's not hun, if he can resist my charms, then he's safe from some two-bit blonde bimbo. If you'd like some help with a quick costume, we can go to my place. I have a dominatrix costume! — only lightly used."

"Gee thanks Andy. Besides, if it's anything like what you're wearing now I doubt I'd fit into it!"

"Yeah, you're probably right. I've done Pilates seven days a week for the past ten years to achieve this Adonis body." Andy gloated as he sucked in his stomach.

"Andy — I just want things to remain the same with me and Mark... Why do I feel so anxious about him getting upset with me?"

"Well you're in luck, forget about the costume, tonight I'm your party godmother. What do *you* want to do tonight?"

"All I'm asking... is that you help me get drunk tonight! Then bring me to Denny's during the wee hours of the morning." I giggled but I wasn't joking.

"Sounds like a plan! I'll get the drinks hun. But, uhm… Seriously, Denny's? Girl! You have lost all self-respect." Andy smirked as we left for the party.

The moment we arrived at the party Andy was getting a lot of attention for his seductive costume. As we got closer to the bar, I couldn't believe who I was seeing. Mark was standing by a group of three lads.

"Andy! Look, Mark's here!"

"Well what are you doing' standing here? Go get your boyfriend!"

"He's probably still mad at me… I need a drink first!"

Andy and I each got a shot of tequila. I surprised even myself as I downed the shot and slammed the glass back onto the bar counter, wiping my mouth with the back of my hand. I started walking towards Mark.

I focused my eyes on where Mark was standing like a hawk locking onto its prey. He right away noticed me coming towards him and gave me a warm and welcoming smile. I smiled back, eager to come closer and kiss my man at last. I was just a few yards away from Mark as we locked eyes while I was walking towards him. Suddenly, a tall blonde chick came and stood right next to Mark. She touched his arm looking like she was asking him some flirty question. At first, I held back a bit but then proceeded to walk closer with a lurched stomach. My warm smile transformed into an awkward grin, but Mark and I were still gazing at each other. Besides, he didn't seem to be listening to whatever the blonde girl was saying as he started walking to meet me halfway. We stared at each other with an apologetic look that not even a thousand words could express.

He wrapped his arms around me and hugged me tight without saying a word. I looked up to meet his eyes as I tried to hold back my tears. Mark kissed me on the lips and hugged me tighter than ever.

"I've missed you, babe…" Mark whispered into my ear.

Before I could even respond, Mark gently took my hand and led me out the door. We stood just outside the bar near this majestic oak tree, with the warm glow of the streetlamps lighting the area.

"I'm sorry, I overreacted. I know you wouldn't do anything I should be worried about." Mark murmured.

"You're right, you have nothing to be worried about. I'm sorry too, babe. I don't know why I act so foolish and inconsiderate sometimes." I threw my hands around Mark's neck, "I've missed you. I don't ever want to fight with you."

"I don't want that either. I couldn't think straight all day. All I could think about is you. I thought I completely lost my mind when I saw you inside."

"Then why weren't you answering my phone calls all day?" I chaffed.

"I'm not going to lie — I was pretty upset earlier. I left my phone in the car so I wouldn't be tempted to fight with you and say things I would regret later."

"I was worried about you..." I murmured as I looked into his eyes.

"I'm sorry, babe. I was just being stubborn... I shouldn't have said those things..." Mark wrapped his arms around me. We walked back in together and approached Andy who was already flirting with some guy in bare chested Tarzan costume.

"So, you see, my costume can come off all at once with one pull of the — Oh, hello there, witch!" Andy said goodbye to his new friend and turned to me. He toggled my witch hat and then looked at Mark perplexed. "So, you didn't bother with a costume either, Mr. Gorgeous? Not even some eyeliner?"

Mark slowly reached behind his back and pulled out this brown hat attached with a stampede string. He put the hat on and instantly looked like a hot cowboy.

"Not quite, I've got a hat!" Mark smirked then looked at me, miming throwing a lasso in the air.

"I see, ever the creative one as well. You two are made for each other!" Andy chuckled then took a sip of his Cosmo rolling his eyes.

The tall blonde girl from earlier approached Mark and whispered something into his ear as she touched his arm. Mark noticed that I was getting uncomfortable and started moving away from her. She was wearing a white slutty nurse costume complete with garter stockings, nurse cap, fake stethoscope, and seven-inch patent leather platform shoes.

"Uh, Stacey, this is my girlfriend, Emma." Mark introduced me as he squeezed my shoulders and clutched my body closer to him. "Stacey was in a few of my classes last year."

"Nice to meet you." I tried to meet Stacey's eyes as I extended my right hand. She only looked at Mark and acted as if she didn't hear what I said or saw me try to shake hands with her.

"Cool. So, Mark... Are we going to dance or what? I've been looking all over for you!" Stacey grabbed Mark's arm and tried to drag him to the dance floor.

"Well, I think I'm just going to chill here with Emma If that's okay." Mark protested as he pulled his arm free from Stacey's grip.

"Oh, c'mon! At least buy me a drink? Pretty please... And take me home tonight! I don't have a ride." Stacey pleaded, pouting her lips like some slutty little brat.

This bitch is testing my patience. I may look calm, but in my mind I've slapped her three times.

Mark looked stunned and didn't know how to respond.

"Um, I'll go get us drinks..." Mark focused his gaze at me. "Babe, what would you like?"

"I'll have a beer--".

"Vodka Cranberry for me... pretty please, cowboy! " I stood there shocked as she interrupted me and winked at Mark reaching for his hand.

Mark slowly walked away towards the bar counter, a befuddled look on his face. Andy raised his eyebrow as Stacey ogled Mark like I was not right next to her.

"So, Stacey... here you go!" Andy put a card into her hands.

"What's this?!" Stacey furrowed her eyebrows inspecting the card.

"It's a cab company you can call so you won't have to ask another girl's boyfriend to bring you home tonight."

"Thanks, but unlike you I'm hot enough to get a ride with a real man, like Mark"

"Excuse me?" Andy blurted out. "Hunny, I'm sure you'll be able to get a ride by some poor, unknowing gentleman with that two-dollar outfit and a perfume that I can only assume is called 'desperate' based on the smell. Hun, I'm only looking out for you, take a cab and have some self-respect." He put his right hand on his waist as he finished and winked at me. Stacey's mouth was wide open in shock and embarrassment.

Mark came back with a bottle of Corona and a vodka cranberry cocktail. He handed me the beer and as he turned to Stacey, Andy swiftly took the vodka cranberry from his hand.

"I'll take the vodka cran, be a shame to waste it... Stacey, shouldn't you be off prospecting gold somewhere, I don't think Mark's rich enough for your taste," Andy moved his neck from side to side like he was ready to pull another gal's weave.

"Uhm, whatever," Stacey stammered as she walked away.

"Bye girl, miss you already" Andy said sarcastically as he waved and sipped Stacey's cocktail.

I loved how Andy played this. There was no better way to put this woman in her place. As Andy looked back at me I mouthed 'Thank You'. Andy's my ride or die friend. I just hoped I could pay him back one day.

Mark and I left the building and walked our way to the parkade. His car was the only one left at the fourth level corner row. We only had a couple of drinks each but the heat between us was unbearable. As we got inside the car he started the ignition and played romantic, slow acoustic songs I'd never heard before.

He looked at me like he just witnessed magic. His brown eyes glimmered like the bright stars in the sky. My heart was thumping, I can't explain the intoxicating desire I was feeling as I locked eyes with him. All my senses were heightened and I could feel my knees weaken.

Slowly, little by little, our bodies traversed towards each other. I instinctively closed my eyes as I reached my hands to stroke Mark's chin. Our lips touched, planting soft kisses that ignited golden sparks between us. As we kissed, I slowly sucked on Mark's bottom lip, it was like sucking on the nectar of some delicate fruit, my soul stirring. We kissed to the rhythm of euphoric music, it was pure love. Passion so exhilarating and yet so calm.

I sighed as our hearts raced and our breathing synchronized. We found ourselves hurriedly undressing each other like presents on Christmas morning.

My body released a burst of adrenaline that aroused my need for his deep touch. Mark leaned more to my side pinning my hands above my head, and against the soft cushion of the passenger's seat. He reached for the lever of my chair and extended its backrest flat towards the backseats. He crossed the center console of his car to be closer to my body. Mark was on top of me, as he gently nibbled on the sides of my neck and shoulders. I felt dampness in between my legs.

He turned me around so that we were both facing the backseat of the car. He was behind me like a sturdy tree protecting me from the weathering storm. Mark lightly ran his hands on my shoulders as he planted kisses on my bare skin. He unhooked my bra, and let it fall effortlessly down onto the seat. He slowly traced his soft lips at the nape of my neck, shooting electrifying shocks down my spine. I felt hot excitement as Mark lowered my thong and traced his fingers inside me. He must have felt how much I wanted him, all of him... right then and there without a care in the world.

I felt him lean against me, his hot breath on my neck as he gently let himself inside me. I was transported to another universe as if my soul had left my body to go to heaven. Every thrust ignited a natural high as we breathed heavily with closed eyes. I didn't want this moment to stop. We both moaned and groaned in euphoric pleasure as we hit the peak of our sensual intimacy. I felt Mark expel all his energy as we breathed heavily with our hearts beating and our pulse palpitating. He took a deep breath and surrendered his body in exhaustion against mine, kissing my cheek. He whispered, "I love you, Emma... so much..." and enclosed his arms against my waist to hold me tight. "I love you so much, Mark..." I mumbled and kissed his cheek in return.

Mark lifted his head to peer if anyone was close by. He jolted up as he took my clothes to try to cover me.

"Babe, someone's coming! Quick, put your clothes on!" He grabbed his jeans and put his pants back on in ten seconds flat. My heart was racing as the thought of getting nearly caught was both exciting and completely embarrassing at the same time. It was the parking guard — he was slowly approaching our car as Mark managed to start the engine and reversed it back out to leave the parkade. Mark's car screeched as he drove away without looking back.

The exhilarating turn of events from a serene, erotic experience to an embarrassing getaway escape was quite a ride! Mark and I could not stop laughing as he drove the car while holding my hand. It was like a rollercoaster ride in a carnival fair, waiting to be re-lived at every opportunity that came.

I met with Mark the next day for a coffee date. He seemed unusually happy and excited as he arrived. We ordered coffee and sat down. Whatever it was, I couldn't wait to hear the good news.

"Babe, you look so giddy! Did you win the lottery?" I surveyed his face for a hint.

"Get this, babe... I finally may have a chance to work side by side with this director I've been following. I had done some work on a few of his television commercial gigs, and he really liked me! We've been in contact here and there for about a year now and I had asked him if he knew about any upcoming projects – he said he has one coming up soon and he'd have a film editing job for me!"

"Wait, a paid filming gig! Babe! That's awesome!" I hugged Mark as we both celebrated the good news. Mark had been struggling lately to find work in film so this was definitely a good thing!

"He's supposed to call soon to officially confirm that I got the job. He said he wasn't sure about the details but would let me know."

"Awesome, you'll definitely get it, babe! If he doesn't hire you, he'll kick himself when you receive an Oscar one day." I chuckled teasing Mark.

After what seemed like an eternity Mark's phone finally rang. He answered it excitedly on the first ring.

"Hello?

Yes, yes...

Great, never been better!

Thank you, man...

That's wonderful!...

Well, yes of course!"

Mark was swaying, his voice sounded thrilled, I was beaming with pride. His face was lit up in excitement until he stopped moving. His face drew in and he was abruptly silent as if he'd just been dealt a bad hand. As he started speaking it sounded like he was trying to be happy and confident, but I could tell that something was off.

"Alright, man...

Yes, please email me the paperwork and I'll look over it.

Thanks again. Can I call you back, say tomorrow?"

Mark ended the call and glanced at me for a moment, he seemed speechless as if he was stalling to relay the news.

"So, you got the job, babe?" I finally said.

Mark slowly nodded but he didn't exude the same excitement he had earlier. He was silent, avoiding eye contact with me. Taking a deep breath, he put his hand between his brows. I waited until Mark was ready to talk while I studied his face. I was curious and worried about what he was mulling over.

"Babe, there's something important I've got to tell you..." Mark had a dumbfounded look. He pressed his lips then covered his mouth with his tightly closed fist.

"What is it babe? What's wrong? You can tell me..." I assured Mark although I wasn't really sure if I could handle the news he'd been hesitating to say.

"The editor job would require me to move to LA for at least six months, but maybe more... They want me to fly there soon." Mark said bitterly as he turned his back on me and swiftly brushed his eyes with the back of his hand. I stood there stupefied. Time slowed down and I couldn't hear anything else but this ringing in my ears. Suddenly, there was a lump in my throat. I tried to take a deep breath and swallow, but it didn't help. My eyes were clouded, and my vision was just a blur. I could feel the tears welling up, ready to breach like unwavering water from a tumultuous river. Mark and I stood a foot away from each other. The silence was deafening, the sound of something you didn't want to hear but needed to be said. I slowly moved closer to him and wrapped my arms around his waist, tightening my grip as if begging him to stay.

CHAPTER SEVEN

Get Up and Get Out

Mark ran his fingers through my hair and pulled me tight to his chest. I looked up at him in a daze and I felt myself trembling a bit, fearing what was to come. There's a woeful expression on his face that made my stomach turn over. I darted my eyes desperately at the floor and clenched my fists tightly at my sides. He took a deep breath and swallowed hard.

"Emma, You know I don't want to leave you but..." Mark trailed off as he stared into my eyes, teary-eyed.

"But this is what you've always wanted to do..." I murmured.

"Yes," Mark finally said after a long pause. "I've wanted this job for years. This may be my only shot. And... Emma, It's only six months..."

"Six months, or more! A lot could happen in six months, Mark! What if you end up falling for another girl in LA? What if you cheat on me!"

"Babe, I love you! I only want to be with you! Do you really think I would ever cheat?"

"No, I mean, I don't know...you'd be far away and I couldn't even check on you..."

"Check on me? Don't you trust me? What about you? Can I trust you while I'm away?" Mark furrowed his brow, his tone sounded like it was more of a statement than a question.

"Me? You think... Well I guess we don't know each other that well then!" I said sarcastically as I looked away.

"If we have no trust, we have no relationship." Mark's voice was stern.

"Yeah, I agree! So, I think we should just end this." My stomach lurched as the words fell out of my mouth. I felt a big lump in my throat start to form.

"What are you saying, Emma? Are you breaking up with me?" Mark murmured as he held my hand. His eyes were morose as he pressed his lips tight.

"Yes, Mark. We're through..." My tears drenched my cheeks. I couldn't hold them back anymore.

Mark was silent, his body seemed paralyzed as he failed to move an inch. He took a deep breath in, expressing some deep frustration. He swallowed. His eyes were fixated on the floor. I grabbed my stuff and started to walk away from Mark.

"Emma---"

I found myself running and not looking back. I ran as if my life depended on it. I felt the need to exhaust myself, to stop feeling pain. Dark clouds were looming in the sky above as rain started to pour down on me while I ran as if to serenade my pain and anguish.

I was wearing a pair of white pants, beige knit sweater, and white sneakers. The splash of muddy water from the puddles and driving cars soiled my clothes as I continued to run as fast as I could.

Completely oblivious of where I was going, I just ran straight ahead without any thought. Drenched from all the rain, abruptly, there was the scariest thunder resounding in the sky. Lightning struck from afar piercing the air around it. *How did I get to an open field by the highway?* My mind raced as I looked around, struggling to find some landmark.

I was still crying, tears rolled down my cheeks mixing with the drowning pour of the rain. I screamed at the top of my lungs. I screamed until my throat gave up and I could no longer let out any sound. My legs surrendered and I slid down into the mucky part of the dirt road, but I couldn't care less. As I laid there in the mud, I rested my head against the earth letting the rain soak me, my entire body on the dirt road next to the fields. And just when I thought the rain would never let up, it stopped. The rain had passed. I got my head up and sat up on the muddy road. Wrapping my arms around my legs, I buried my head down into my knees. I had never felt so alone. I closed my eyes and thought over my now-ended relationship with Mark. Through rose-colored glasses, I dwelled on all our amazing moments together. Moments that I thought I would never forget but we would never share again. I looked far towards the edge of the horizon and sobbed some more, a deep heave mourning my lost Mark.

I looked down, checking my phone for the time. I had numerous texts and missed calls from Mark. He was worried. I knew I shouldn't have run away. My mind and entire body were exhausted. I walked to the closest street sign I could find. My legs were aching, and I was starting to feel a chill from the wind whipping at my rain-soaked body. I called Laura and told her what had just happened. She told me to stay where I was as she hurried to pick me up. Laura was the person I could always call when I'm in trouble. She drove right ahead to where I was without hesitation. She found me sitting on the side of the road waiting to be saved by my best friend. Pulling up, she got out of the car and ran over to me.

"Jesus, Emma! Are you Okay?" Laura inspected me head to toe.

"I'm okay, I'm just a little cold..." I murmured as I threw my arms around her. I started to cry, sobbing in her arms.

"Get inside the car... I've brought a change of clothes for you... There's a blanket in the car too." Laura opened the passenger seat. I sat in the car shivering, relieved with warmth and shelter. Laura looked at me and gave me tissues to clean up my face.

"You look like you got washed up from a shipwreck!" Laura snickered in an attempt to make me laugh.

"It's my new look, a touch of boho, like bohemian-y?" I murmured desperately, trying to make light of the situation.

"Same thing!" Laura bantered instantly.

I checked my text messages. Mark was worried about me and wanted to talk. I wanted to let him know that I was fine, so I told him that I was with Laura. We agreed to meet the next day. I didn't speak while Laura was driving, I just stared blankly at the road. Tears rolled down my cheeks as I tried to use my sweater sleeves to wipe them. Flashbacks of Mark and I driving around, laughing, and having the best times of our lives were right before my eyes. Laura didn't say a word, letting me have my moment of grief. I rested my head against the window and covered my mouth, I didn't want to be home alone that night.

"Stay at my place tonight. I have a tub of ice cream that will drown all your troubles away." Laura said as if she could read my mind.

"Okay..." I whispered, wiping another batch of tears that flowed down like Niagara Falls.

I spent the night at Laura's place hugging a tub of ice cream then eventually fell asleep next to it. She had a two-bedroom apartment which she shared with her sister, Becky, who was abroad for the time being, so I had her bed all to myself. I woke up the next morning disgusted by the sticky ice cream which had melted onto my cheeks and fingers. I had finished an entire gallon of vanilla bean ice cream all by myself. It was not one of my proudest moments. I was officially a cliché – a sobbing woman, binge-eating ice cream out of the pail while listening to Adele's hits after a breakup.

The next day, I let Mark know that I was at Laura's place if he still wanted to meet. About half an hour later, I heard him pull up outside to pick me up. I thanked Laura for her hospitality just before I left, gathering my wits about me to have the conversation I had been dreading all night. Mark and I were both silent as I opened his car door and sat in. He drove over and pulled into the closest quiet park. We walked along a peaceful path towards a lone bench. Most of the trees had shed their leaves by this time with winter on its way, a cessation of our idyllic romance. As we sat down, I took a deep breath, taking in all the gloominess of the wind. Mark held my hand and locked his eyes on me.

"I love you so much..." Mark started to whisper as he gazed at me.

"Mark---"

"Wait, I want you to know that I will always love you, Emma." I let myself into Mark's arms and rested my head on his chest, his hand still holding mine.

"Will you meet with me in six months?" Mark continued. "Maybe circumstances will have changed – maybe I'll have enough money by then... and we could move in together – maybe even in LA, then in a few years... maybe we could get married, have kids... grow old together... maybe we'll have grandkids..." he trailed off sounding hopeful yet disarrayed.

"Stop it. I'll meet with you in six months..." I tightened my grip on Mark's hand. Mark and I fixated on the leafless trees in front of us. I settled my head onto his shoulder as we sat there in silence for a while.

"I'll be dreaming of the day we see each other again." Mark looked hopeful as he threw his arms around me. I nodded as I gazed at him with a wistful look in my eyes. Never before had six months seemed like an eternity.

Later that week Mark flew off to Los Angeles. Before he left, we made a pact to give each other space since we'd broken up. No calling or texting unless it's an absolute emergency. We also decided that no matter what we would remain friends, even if we didn't end up together in six months.

After he left, I bought a few bottles of cheap wine and quarantined myself to my apartment. I called in sick at work for a few days missing my classes in school as well. I spent most of my days sleeping in and barely moving. I ate more chocolate and ice cream than ever before. Each day's dinner consisted of an extra large pizza just for myself along with greasy breadsticks and chicken wings. My sink accumulated piles of dirty dishes. I didn't bother cleaning my place nor did I do any laundry. Dirty clothes and garbage were scattered everywhere. Adele and Sam Smith's entire discography was on repeat and shuffle. I turned my phone off since all I would end up doing otherwise was look at the pictures or videos of Mark and me. I desperately wanted to call or text him. To see if he missed me too. I fantasized that he had been desperately texting and calling me, trying to get a hold of me — that he wanted to return and missed me so much. I felt like an addict going through withdrawal. I tried to psych myself up by listening to Bobby McFerrin's *Don't Worry Be Happy* record only to succumb to Al Green's *How Can You Mend a Broken Heart?* And just when I thought I was too tired to sob because my eyes had dried up, I found the good old *One Last Cry* anthem by Brian McKnight. I liked old school heartbreak songs because they're more sentimental. I might as well get on with the heartbreak classics that had stood the test of time.

I was about to rewind my sappy tunes when I heard a familiar knock on the door. I knew exactly who it was. Laura and I had a secret knock like some code to get inside a dingy speakeasy tucked away in a dark alley. I tried ignoring it, hoping that she would just leave thinking I wasn't there, but Laura was probably the most persistent person I've ever known. She stood by my door for at least half an hour continuously knocking and calling my name. She knew I was home wasting my life.

I slightly opened the door and peered through the small gap. I didn't want company, I just wanted to be alone and sulk for a few more days. Laura pushed the door wide open without difficulty as I was too weak to even protest it.

"What's happening to you? Your phone's turned off; I've been trying to call you for at least a few days now! I didn't know if I was going to find my best friend's corpse or..." Laura trailed off, obviously upset.

"I'm fine! Don't be dramatic." I murmured slowly crawling back to bed.

"I can't let you do this to yourself anymore! Your apartment has never been this filthy...And the smell! When was the last time you took a shower?" Laura gave me a disgusted look as she picked up the garbage around my apartment. I buried my head in some pillows under my blanket, trying to avoid listening to her. I fell asleep despite the shuffling movement of swishing, gurgling, and clanking that reverberated across the room. By the time I gained consciousness, my apartment was just how it used to be. Dirty dishes were washed. Trash was emptied and taken out. Dirty clothes were put in the hamper.

"Huh, how long was I out," I mumbled as I sat up in bed.

"Never mind that, now all you need to do is take a shower! Don't make me hose you down!" Laura sounded serious. I appreciated her effort to help clean up after me, and if I'm honest, having a tidy place after a few days of living like a rat started lifting my spirit. It's as if I was being brought back to the light. I took a long warm shower, brushed my teeth and put on fresh pajamas.

"Um, No! You're not wearing that!" Laura commanded me like a drill sergeant. "We're getting out of your apartment!".

"I'm sick..." I protested, feeling like some lazy teenager trying to skip school.

"Well, you're right about one thing: You are sick. And the cure – is to see the light of day. You're living like a vampire! But without any of the power, strength, or sexual prowess."

"I need sleep..." I laid down and covered my body with a blanket.

Laura turned on my phone and gave it to me. As I checked my text messages, I held on to the hope that I would see something from Mark. Any indication, even a glint, that he was suffering as I had been — that it was all a big mistake and he was on his way back. But there was nothing from him. Not even to see how I was doing. My fevered hopes had been broken and crashed against reality; it was not a pretty sight.

I saw that Jason had sent me a couple of messages letting me know that my laptop was fixed, and that he could drop it off at my place sometime in the afternoon. I replied apologizing for not getting back to him sooner. I gave him my address and a time for us to meet later.

Laura was right, I had to get my life back together. Mark didn't even text me at all the entire time I was mourning our breakup. I felt as if he no longer cared, but I also realized that we had agreed to not contact each other until after six months. I was tired of crying, tired of listening to depressing music, and tired of eating greasy, unhealthy food. My back was aching from lying down for too long. I was just tired of it all.

I decided I would go out somewhere with Laura. She listened to me talk over and over about Mark. I realized how selfish I had been. I hadn't even asked her about what was going on in her life. I right away shifted the topic to her. It was then that I noticed her face lit up and she got excited talking about her long-time boyfriend, Richard. When I started focusing my attention to Laura, I forgot my own woes.

Maybe this is an opportunity for me to focus on myself and start acting on things that I wanted to accomplish. Mark is chasing af-

ter his dream, I should probably do the same for myself – whatever that may be.

After Laura dropped me off at my apartment, I stood waiting in the front lobby for Jason. I saw him pull up and park his car in front of my building. He walked to the main door where I met him.

"Hey, Jason... Thanks so much for doing this, I really appreciate it..." My eyes were still puffy and my voice was a bit sheepish and soft.

"Don't mention it. Here you go." Jason reached out and handed my laptop.

"Thanks, and here's your payment, as promised..." I gave Jason a pack of Mr. Big chocolate bars I had picked up with Laura earlier.

Jason grinned and he looked pleased, but I still felt like I owed him so much more.

"Why, thank you! I wasn't really expecting anything, but this should save me a trip to the vending machine for the next few days."

"That's the least I can do..."

"Are you feeling okay? Have you been sick lately? Jason asked, surveying my face.

"Yeah sort of... Uhm, I really can't thank you enough, Jason. Can I buy you a cup of coffee?" I forced a smile, quickly changing the subject.

"Yeah, for sure, that'd be nice." Jason looked at me with smiling eyes.

"There's a bookstore just three blocks from here with a coffee shop inside it. We could walk from here."

"Sounds great! Just give me a couple of minutes and I'll be right out." I hurried back inside, left my laptop and quickly glanced at myself in the mirror to make sure I didn't have awful racoon eyes.

Jason was a perfect gentleman. He opened doors for me and even walked on the side of oncoming traffic as if he was a royal guard protecting me. He had the posture of an army officer and the mind of a chess master. He exuded respect and chivalry. Whenever he spoke, I looked up to him as if he was decoding the Da Vinci code.

As we roamed around the bookstore, I wandered through the autobiography shelf and found Ernest Hemingway's '*A Moveable Feast*'. Picking it up off the shelf, I started reading and by the time I was done the first few pages, I was hooked. I had to have it.

" 'If you are lucky enough to have lived in Paris as a young man, then wherever you go for the rest of your life, it stays with you, for Paris is a moveable feast'," Jason recited those famous lines to me with ease and confidence.

"I'm guessing this is one of your recommended books?" I bantered as we roamed the literary classics shelves.

"Easily one of my top three." Jason raised his eyebrows and nodded as if I needed more convincing to buy the book.

"His memoir epitomized Paris as *the* city where creative minds congregate during the roaring twenties. It was the book that romanticized being a starving brilliant writer in the most beautiful city in the world." Jason articulated this, speaking as if from experience.

"I wish I could go to Paris one day and write for a living like he did." I murmured.

"You should write. Why don't you?" Jason uttered with conviction.

"Well, I mean it's not that easy. I've never written anything before besides school papers. And regardless, I can't afford to go to Paris. One can only dream, I guess."

"You'd be surprised... how dreams can come true. It's all up to you." Jason said plainly, he sounded like a fairy-tale narrator ending a magical story.

"I sure hope so--" I trailed off while we walked towards the cashier.

"I'll just grab something quick. I'll see you upstairs for coffee?" He pointed up to our meeting place as he slowly walked back.

"Okay sounds good, what do want to drink?" I rushed saying before he was out of sight.

"I'll have a black coffee. Thanks!"

I chose a small table with two chairs opposite each other overlooking the massive bookstore from the floor above. I ordered a latte for myself, and a black coffee for Jason. As I watched him riding the escalator up to the café, I noticed how he stood a lot taller than most people. He was about six foot three, with lean, slender body, alabaster skin, and dark blonde hair.

"Hey, sorry for the wait... Oh, thanks for the coffee!" Jason sat down across from me and took a sip.

"No biggie! Actually — I should probably buy you coffee for a week all things considered!"

"Nonsense, I wouldn't allow that... Twenty-four Mr. Big chocolate bars would have sufficed." Jason grinned as he handed me a paper bag.

"What's this?" I asked bemused. I peeked inside as I took out a dark brown leather notebook with writing on the front cover that said 'IN ORDER TO WRITE ABOUT LIFE, FIRST YOU MUST LIVE IT. –HEMINGWAY'.

"Wow – this is a beautiful notebook!" I ran my hands through the covers admiring its exquisite craftsmanship.

"I got it for you. I hope you'll fill the pages with rich and unforgettable memories." Jason smiled at me while staring at my shocked face.

"What? But, Jason... You didn't have to..."

"I know..." Jason raised his cup in mock toast, " 'Emma, I think this is the beginning of a beautiful friendship'," Jason pressed his lips trying to suppress his visible smile while we clinked our cups.

"Ha! You're kidding! You like Casablanca too?" I laughed, amazed at how Jason and I both seemed to like the same classic movie and it's most famous line.

He and I talked like old friends for hours until the bookstore closed that night. He was very interesting and charismatic, he could easily explain in detail — subjects on world history, scientific theories, or anything that had to do with technology. To say that he was smart was an understatement.

Later on, when I got home, I checked my Instagram account. I noticed I had a message from someone I didn't know. It read:

Hello Emma,

My name is Jackson Gallagher. I found your Instagram account through your video for a fundraising event where you sang. I wanted to say that you have an excellent voice. That video captioned your name as Emma Bray. I'm reaching out to you to see if you know anyone by the name of Marilyn Bray? She's now Marilyn Gallagher but Bray was her maiden name. I hope you can respond. I'm looking for my sister.

Thanks,

Jackson

CHAPTER EIGHT

Oh Brother & Brooch

Marilyn Bray. How could I forget the name, she was my grandparents' only child. She was also the heartless woman who abandoned her daughter to escape the difficulties of being a mother. She pretended I didn't exist for twenty-three years, so why start now?

I was upset, I didn't get to have a mother or a father growing up so when my grandparents passed on, I no longer had a family. It made me want to hate my mother. But I couldn't. Not in any real sense of the term. I think what I was really feeling was fear and not hate. I guess I was just trying to protect myself from getting hurt. I feared that she would be disappointed in me after we met. What if she was hoping I looked better, or was more successful or fiercely intelligent?

I let out a sigh as I replied back to Jackson's message and agreed to meet him at a local brewery near my apartment called *Two for the Road*. I figured I may as well see what he wanted, I could always leave after all. I came a bit earlier than our agreed time so I could have a drink before we got into talking. I was nervous and uneasy, so the alcohol helped calm my nerves.

Jackson finally arrived and walked towards my table. I recognized him from his Instagram photo, and I assumed he recognized me as well as he walked right over to me. I waved my hand as he made his way in my direction. He was wearing a light blue oxford button-down shirt, topped with a navy blazer with silk striped pocket squares, khaki-colored chinos with the ends cuffed up, and leather penny loafers sans socks. His highly polished look was accessorized with a black leather watch and a brown leather belt. I wondered if he dressed like a Ralph Lauren model every day. He was about five feet ten inches tall, with clean-shaven face and slick back dark hair. He looked like Jude Law from The Talented Mr. Ripley.

"Emma, it's so nice to finally see you in the flesh!" Jackson extended both of his arms for a hug.

I welcomed his embrace as I felt obligated, but I was like a rock unable to move or at least respond to his warm gesture. Instead, I nodded in affirmation with a half-smile as I fixated my eyes on the floor.

Trying to look unfazed, I felt a twinge of envy for Jackson. All his life, he had a happy family, and I was an orphan. I knew these thoughts weren't fair because he had nothing to do with how my life turned out, but I just couldn't help feeling jealous of his perfect life.

We ordered pale ales on tap, a veggie burger for him, and a classic Reuben sandwich for me. We passed the awkward *how are you's* and the typical weather report small talk. The embarrassing silence between us was deafening as we munched on our meals.

"We've been looking for you for a few years now," Jackson said finally after some silence. "Mom hired a private investigator, but nothing turned up until recently. You were kind of hard to track. It's when I saw your video that I found you on the Internet. You have a golden voice, sis!"

"Thank you... Wait, you guys were looking for me?" I was stupefied.

"Yes… When did you move away from Langley? The private investigator said our grandpa passed years ago. You and grandma then moved to an apartment. Then when grandma passed on, you left but didn't tell your neighbors where you were moving to. All we had was a picture of you and grandma from your old neighbor."

"I didn't think anybody would look for me."

"Emma, you're my sister. We're family. Family's supposed to be there for each other." Jackson expressed a caring look on his face.

"Huh--- Yeah, you would think!" I cackled. "So how's it like to be raised in a perfect family?" I goaded unprovoked, sounding like some bitter evil half-sister.

"It wasn't exactly perfect, Emma. I know what mom had done…" Jackson stopped himself before stating the obvious. "And I think it's shameful and absolutely despicable! I'll give her the chance to tell you her story. But, growing up… I was sent to a boarding school. Our mother was not really the nurturing type. I was not raised in a perfect family. Mom was always working while dad racked up frequent flyer miles on business trips. Then, when I was sixteen, mom and dad got divorced."

"I'm sorry to hear that, must have been hard…" I mumbled.

"Thanks, it was. I wish we grew up together. I hope it's not too late." Jackson took a deep breath and grinned with a hopeful look in his eyes.

I did not want to disappoint Jackson, so I smiled and nodded while taking a swig of beer in my hand.

"So, what are you taking in school?" I tried to change the subject into something that did not have anything to do with me.

"Political Science – as my Pre-Law. Just following mom's footsteps."

"She's a lawyer?" I was baffled. I succeeded in covering my mouth before I almost spat out the beer on Jackson's face.

"Yeah, she is. Dad's a lawyer too... they met in law school, didn't our grandparents tell you? Anyway, but dad... he ventured into oil business and that's what made our lives more comfortable so to speak." Jackson seemed embarrassed admitting he was born with a silver spoon in his mouth.

Of course, I didn't know what my mother did for a living because I barely knew her! My grandparents didn't talk much about my mother at all. They were probably just as dismayed that their daughter dumped her own child. I abruptly didn't want to know anything more about my mother or her family. If she was well off with a decent career, then why the hell did she not come back for me? *I couldn't help but think.*

This information angered me. She was not a helpless young woman who had nothing to offer her child. She was totally capable of raising me. She simply did not want me in her life. I didn't understand why I was feeling this way but I felt years of bitterness rising up inside me. I still wanted to pretend that she had to have a really good reason as to why she left me — that she did not have a choice. That glimmer of hope had vanished.

"Would you consider meeting with mom soon? She wants to see you, Emma. Please let me take you to see her." Jackson pleaded as I looked away and took a deep breath. I took a sip of my beer and finished it off, delaying my response as Jackson patiently waited.

"I don't know... this is all happening too fast. Maybe I should think about it for a while and get back to you." I muttered pretending to check my phone for important messages.

"We've wasted too much time thinking and not doing anything, Emma! I think it's about time to face the truth, make peace and forgive..."

"It's just that I don't know who she is! She's a stranger to me! No, she's worst than that, I can't imagine any stranger who would abandon their own child!" I said with disgust. "Look Jackson, I'm not able to just instantly forgive and forget that she left me at birth because she suddenly had a change of heart!"

My head was throbbing in pain. I felt my stomach involuntarily attempting to heave out the food I just consumed. I resigned to bury my head in my hands. I felt like I was strapped to a chair whilst looking at an open door, desperate to escape.

"Okay, Emma. I understand. I'm sorry... I was too persistent. Just take all the time you need until you're ready." Jackson moved over to the chair next to me and patted my shoulder. He asked the waiter for a glass of water and gave it to me.

"Thanks, I really appreciate you Jackson, I know you didn't do anything to cause this and that you're only trying to help. It's just hard for me, I need some time to think about everything." I relaxed and gave Jackson a big hug.

"For sure sis, I get it. Call me anytime... If you ever need anything..." he hugged me back as we said our goodbyes.

I walked around my neighborhood aimlessly for almost an hour until I finally made it home. I was more upset than ever. I thought about how she even missed both of my grandparents' funerals! There was absolutely no way she could make up for twenty-three years of absence!

I needed some time to divert my attention to something else that would calm me down. I decided I would distract myself by reading my new book, Hemingway's *A Moveable Feast*. I picked it up and sat down in my comfy reading chair with my warm blanket and some tea.

As I read, I felt myself mesmerized and fascinated by Hemingway's account of his time in Paris in the nineteen twenties when he was a struggling writer living in a tiny apartment with his wife. I had always dreamed of becoming a writer. I thought that I needed to formally learn how to write before I could even create anything good enough. I figured that I could not possibly be called a writer without sufficient education. So, after high school, I decided to attend University to learn the fundamentals of writing and literature. I had taken out student loans to fund my schooling and I worked as a waitress. I was only able to take a few courses per semester since I had to work to earn enough to cover all my bills.

Now I am in my final year and graduation is just a few months away. Why am I more scared than ever? Did I really think that attaining a degree is going to guarantee me a bright future? I have not traveled anywhere, nor tried to pursue my dream of becoming a writer by actually starting to write.

I realized that putting off the actual work was not going to be an option anymore. I was no longer allowed to use my ignorance as an excuse not to start a career.

I feared the future... scared of things I did not understand. Most of all, I was scared that one day, my life would be over but I never truly experienced how to live.

As I finished the book, I was inspired to go out in the world and explore both the beauty and mystery of an adventure. To keep moving and trying no matter where I was standing.

One day, I'll visit Paris. I would love to get lost in the city of lights until my feet couldn't move an inch anymore. I wonder if that will be possible in this lifetime.

Later that week, Andy came to my apartment to hang out. He had already gone on a shopping spree, but shockingly, he said it wasn't satisfying him anymore. I asked him to help me find things in my apartment to sell online. I laid out all the items I would be willing to part with and watched him pick up each one with a bemused interest of an antique dealer.

"So, you have some *interesting* pieces around here..." Andy smirked in a slightly condescending tone.

"Oh yeah? I didn't know you fancy thrift store and garage sale items!" I bantered in a snap.

"Hmm, well my parents love to buy old weird stuff in auctions. My dad once bought Andrew Carnegie's lock of hair for the bargain price of fifteen grand! And my mom won Marilyn Monroe's old brassiere for only twenty-five g's – can you believe it? Such a steal!" Andy shook his head and scrutinized my thrift finds.

"Well, they're welcome to a lock of my hair and one of my old brassieres, and I'd settle for a tenth of what they paid," I joked while Andy gave me this bewildered look. "Anyway, the stuff I've picked up was only like a couple of bucks here and there. I did not pay over a hundred bucks for any of these!"

"Oh I know, my dear. I know..." Andy sat down on my rattan peacock chair, a gem I found in an early bird garage sale. He then elegantly crossed his legs and placed his hands on his thighs. He looked like the cover art for *Queen of the Damned*.

I started organizing the random stuff around my apartment that I could sell. There were some white floral teacups, books, bookends, a jewelry box, a bronze tea kettle, a globe and an hourglass.

"So, what do you think about the items I have so far?" I forced a smile, hoping to get some words of encouragement from Andy.

"Uhm, well, how much were you looking to get for this *exquisite* collection?" Andy carefully inspected my antiquities. He lifted each item and peered at them, making a funny face.

"I'm not selling these to you, Andy. I'm gonna sell these on the Internet — maybe Ebay, Craigslist or Kijiji to make a few bucks!" I blurted out defiantly trying to uphold my poise and dignity.

"Yes, well, I certainly wish you all the luck... wait a minute... what do we have here!" Andy held up and scrutinized this green turtle brooch that was inside one of the jewelry boxes. His interest grew as he inspected it closely against the light and gently ran his hands over it.

"Oh, yeah, that brooch was inside that jewelry box when I bought it at the thrift store. I didn't think it was worth anything, you want it?" I nonchalantly glanced at him wondering why he was suddenly interested in some old turtle brooch. It certainly was not a business magnate's lock of hair or some Hollywood bombshell's underwear.

"*Want it*?! I *need* it!" Andy gently presented the brooch in his right palm and slowly sashayed his hips walking towards me like Vanna White from the Wheel of Fortune.

"Oh, well then you can have it! My gift to you!" I clapped his back and moved my hand as if dismissing his overt enthusiasm.

"What? No, No, No! I've been called many things in my life, but I — Andrew Corbin Hawthorne, The Third — will never take advantage of the less fortunate! I mean my God, woman, have you no idea what this is?" Andy stared at me in disbelief, as if I was a peasant.

"Andy, it's just a green turtle brooch someone forgot to take out from the jewelry box. It's a freebie!"

"Well, I can't blame you... It took me *years* of experience to have a trained eye for the finer things in life." Andy carefully put down the turtle brooch. "Emma, Listen... This looks like a handmade, nineteen forties textured three-dimensional jade turtle brooch. About fourteen karat yellow gold with bright red Ruby eyes and a well-polished natural untreated **Jadeite Jade** shell!" He paused with his hands open as if waiting for my reaction.

"Right, okay... Wait what?! Did you say gold? Like real gold?" I jumped in excitement, finding this little piece of information.

"Uhm, yes... The pin on the back, the turtle's head, its legs and the base of its shell — All real gold. But that's not the point!" Andy shook his head, irritated by my reaction as if he was teaching a toddler how to tie her shoes for the fifteenth time.

"Okay... So, what *IS* the point?" I retorted with a sarcastic grin.

Andy's eyes were bulging as if I dismissed something very important.

"Uhm...***Jadeite?!*** God Emma, do you even listen to me? ***Jadeite Jade!***" Andy exasperated.

"Oh, yeah! Jade's your birthstone! Is that why you're so hysterical? Sorry I momentarily forgot your birthstone!" I said, trying to suppress a smile.

"Well yes, thank you for remembering that it's my birthstone. None of my other friends remember..." Andy softened clasping his hands together.

"What other friends?" I bantered as I threw a pillow at him. My aim was way off, knocking down a fragile floral teacup on the table.

"Okay, but that's not my point, seriously! Do you know how valuable this is? Jadeite protects the wearer and attracts fortune and prestige! It's also a *dream stone* Emma!" Andy said with such enthusiasm as if I knew what that implied.

"Ohhhkay, and what exactly is a *dream stone*, if you could please enlighten me?" I mocked waving my hands around as if I was visiting some gypsy fortune teller.

"It only solves dreams, Emma, *dreams*! And it lets you access the spiritual realm!" Andy exclaimed as he picked up the turtle brooch meticulously once more.

"I see... So, you're into crystal healing, personalized horoscopes, moonstones, tealeaf, tarot, ayahuasca and now *dream stones*?"

"Ugh, some people have all the luck. Anyway, what I'm trying to say is that it's valuable and I would like to purchase it, so sell it to me!" Andy demanded.

"Sell it to you? Andy, you're one of my closest friends! Just take it. Think of it as my token of appre---"

"Babe, it's worth over three thousand dollars! Three thousand five hundred to be exact and I'll buy it from you for just as much!" Andy interrupted as he watched the ungodly shock spread across my face.

"What?! Are you out of your mind! Why would you pay that much for some old turtle pin!" I protested, as I knew firsthand that Andy was a reckless spender when it came to peculiar items, ninety-nine per cent of the population would pass on.

Rolling his eyes Andy took my laptop and went to this website where wealthy people buy hard-to-find antique and pre-loved luxury goods. We found a Jadeite Jade cufflinks selling for *ten thousand, three hundred dollars*. Suddenly, the turtle Jadeite brooch did not seem so unreasonably priced anymore. I mean, not to these chumps.

"See! You're doing me a favor by selling this to me for only thirty-five hundred dollars!" Andy examined the brooch with delicate care as if holding the only antidote to some rare poison afflicting him. "My parents will be so proud of me for scoring this deal! They might even think I swindled my friend for a bargain!" Andy stared off into the distance, likely imagining his parents brimming with pride.

"But what if it's not a real Jadeite Jade Andy! And I... I just got it as a freebie in a jewelry box I picked up from Goodwill!" He was one of my best friends and I would never take advantage of his weakness in buying expensive things.

"Emma don't insult me, I told you, I have a trained eye for the finer things! This is not my first Jadeite Jade! But... if you really want to make sure you're selling me the real thing, I'll send it to GIA for analysis."

"Who's GIA?"

"Gemological Institute--- Well, basically... they do tests in their lab to analyze precious stones and certify their findings in a report. If it turns out to be a real gem, then I'll pay you for it."

Andy never sounded more rational than ever.

"Okay, that sounds fair to me. Don't give me any money until we're absolutely sure!"

"Emma, you've got to relax. Sometimes, good things just happen to good people! Don't feel guilty about it. You've been buying people's trash for years! Don't you think it's about time you found a diamond in the rough?" Andy shook me with his arms extended as he gave me the most encouraging pep talk.

"No…" I protested, shaking my head.

Andy threw his hands in the air like he just lost all faith in humanity.

"I found a Jadeite in the rough!" I corrected, smiling ear to ear as I busted out laughing at my own stupid joke.

"Oh hunny, that's some gentle comedy. You're lucky you're so cute or I would never speak to you again after that!" Andy carefully took my *Jadeite in the rough* and walked away.

CHAPTER NINE

Just Jump!

It was a crisp November night. I just had to gaze at the deep silver full moon gleaming like a shining stone against the cloudless sky. At this hour, all I could do was think about Mark.

Sadness crept up in my chest like thick, toxic smoke slowly choking the life out of me. I sat there wondering if he was thinking about me. If he still cared about me. If he still loved me.

I must have been hypnotized by the moon, because my thoughts had just transported me to places where Mark and I had been together. I still remembered how his eyes glimmered in a glint of the moonlight... how he wrapped his hands around me on a breezy nightfall... how he kissed my lips with gentleness...

Tears started streaming down my cheeks as I remembered our moments of pure joy, passion... love.

Will there ever be a pill to medicate a broken heart? There should be. Because the affliction pulls you helplessly, down to the deep dark abyss, never to be found again. How happy is the blameless vestal's lot indeed. I thought bitterly.

I forced myself to walk back inside my apartment as I tried to pull myself together. I reminded myself that despite all my past misfortunes and failures, I was still standing, still living. I held on to the tiny chance of Mark coming back...

I woke up to Andy's phone call. I answered on the fourth ring as I uttered *'Hello?'* half-awake with a sleep mask partially covering my eyes.

"Wake up, sleepy head! Papa's here!" Andy sounded as giddy as someone playing with Beagle puppies.

"Why are you always interrupting my best dreams?" I muttered.

"Let me in! I have a surprise for you!"

"If it's another snail wrinkle cream Andy, I swear - I'll kill you!" I groaned as I stumbled out of bed.

I harnessed every bit of willpower I could muster to shamble over to my front door. He was cheekier than usual despite being greeted by me.

"Hey babe - My God, you look like the Crypt Keeper! Did you just wake up from some five-thousand-year curse?" Andy laughed as he gazed at me.

"Shut up Andy, what do you want?" I asked, half asleep.

"And those Pajamas, did you raid the lost-and-found for those?"

"Andy -"

"Okay, okay, close your eyes and hand me your palm... No peeking!"

I obeyed, lifting my sluggish arm. I slowly turned my palm up to receive the apparent surprise.

"Now open your eyes!"

I felt a glass container resting in my hand. *Another full jar of snail slime.*

"You woke me up from almost making out with Ryan Gosling for this?" I vented at Andy while I put away his present in my *never-to-be-seen-again* drawer. "Thank you. Although, I might not use it yet — maybe for a very long time."

"Yes, well, judging by the state of things I'm afraid it's too late!" Andy snickered.

"I need to go back to bed. Ryan Gosling might be back and we might finally do it! But don't wake me up this time!" I bounced back into my bed and covered myself with a warm blanket.

"Ryan Gosling?" He said incredulously with a laugh. "Finish your dream girl, you'll see he ends up with me!"

"Eat your heart out Andy, let me get some sleep!" I said into my pillow.

"Hmm, it's time to wake up, because money never sleeps!" Andy declared as he handed me a piece of paper.

I jolted up as soon as I saw the letterhead. 'GIA'

I ran my eyes swiftly to the important sections of the gemo-logical report:

DETAILS
Shape.......................Oval
Transparency.........Translucent
Color.........................Green

TREATMENT
Natural Color. No indications of impregnation.
RESULTS
Species....................Jadeite Jade

When I looked up, Andy was already holding a money gun locked and loaded to make it rain in my apartment. I was jump-ing and yelling, "It's real! It's a Jadeite! It's a Jadeite Jade!"

Andy pulled the trigger, and cash went flying in the air as I twirled like a stripper.

After it emptied, we continued laughing on the floor.

"Andy, why do you have a money gun?" I asked as I contin-ued to laugh.

"Actually, I have two, one I keep in my car for such occasions as this and another I keep on my night stand because, well it doesn't matter, it's mine and I'll do what I want with it" he gave me this devilish smile as we cleaned my apartment.

It was a fun twelve seconds of flying twenty-dollar bills until it was over. I knew Andy well enough to realize that he specifically took twenty-dollar bills to make it rain until happy hour. By the time I was done picking up cash, I had thirty-five hundred dollars that came flying out of nowhere.

I headed out for a swim every now and then at my neighborhood recreation center. That afternoon I did my swim warm-ups, the obligatory flutter kicks, moderate intensity of different swim-strokes, and finally, a cool down swim at an easy pace. As I climbed out of the pool and began walking towards the change room, I took my swim caps and goggles off.

I proceeded to walk while trying to read the time off the clock on the wall.

"It's three--- Ahhhhhhhhhhh!" I screeched as I slipped full-tilt on the wet surface by the side of the pool. A hard impact was menacing. I was about to free-fall on my back and hit my head against the pool-tiled floor. In a nanosecond, I accepted my looming fate as I squeezed my eyes shut.

An unexpected pair of brawny arms abruptly caught my falling body like some guardian angel freeing me from an imminent danger.

I squinted, gingerly unfolding my eyes to discover my savior.

"Jason?" I murmured.

Our eyes met as I was lying in the shelter of his arms like wings of an angel that safeguarded me from my own demise. He lightly loosened his protective grip and flashed a smile of relief.

I cracked a smile too, discombobulated. I could not believe my luck.

"Are you okay? Jason asked concerned, assessing me for any injury with a quick scan of my body from head to toe.

"Yes, I'm fine. Thank you!" I slowly stood up as I glanced at Jason's bare chest. This was the very first time I saw him with nothing on but a complementary grey lace-up board shorts with droplets of water trickling down his skin. My eyes got lost at the sight of his defined muscles and tight core.

Oh My.

I snapped out of my disconcertment. I realized shortly after that Jason had never seen me in a wet swimsuit either. I felt like some grandma who just finished her aquafit class! I doubted that he fancied my toothpick legs sticking out below. I suppose my tush looked decent though.

"I was by the dive pool when I saw you. I thought I'd say *hi* so I started walking towards your way. I was right behind you when you slipped—"

"You don't know how happy I am that you were there! I mean, I could have died!" I did not hold back, throwing a big warm hug around him for his heroism. He gently enfolded me back with his arms like a protective cocoon. I felt his chest heave with deep breathing.

I jerked back the second I felt that we lingered a little longer than we should.

"So, you come here often?" My voice was shrill as I tried to relinquish my awkwardness.

"Yeah, I come here every now and then, they have a nice dive pool and tower over there." Jason pointed at the tower boasting one-meter, three-meter and five-meter diving platforms.

"Do you like to dive?" Jason asked wide-eyed.

"Not really..." I sheepishly shook my head. "I love to swim, but I've never dove or even jumped off from a platform before."

"Never? Why's that? You won't drown!" Jason egged me on with a slight chuckle.

"Well, it's just too high... I would never dare." I sounded like a purebred chicken-shit. "I mean, it's not like I don't want to, but I've never really had the courage I guess"

"Hey, I get it, but I think you should give it a try, at least once before you leave today. But only if you have fully recovered from earlier."

I watched Jason climb up the tower as he sprinted towards the edge of the highest platform. He spun his body before he took a huge leap in the air without any trace of hesitation.

I gazed in silence admiring his unflinching determination to backflip for his final stunt. He plummeted to the deep turquoise chlorinated water, then rose to the surface with a broad smile spread across his face.

Truthfully, I wanted to jump off that tower from the very first day I saw it. I had been to this place many times before, but I never dared to try.

Am I scared of heights? Afraid that a freak accident could happen if I jump? I could have been seriously injured just moments ago from simply walking next to the pool.

The tower looked intimidating from below. I felt as if jumping from it was a rite of passage offered only to those who were brave enough to conquer their fears.

The Fear of the Unknown was taunting me, and I was its slave and it, my master. Fear filled me as if to say, '*You cannot defeat me! I own you! Who do you think you are?*'

Out of the blue, I stood up and decided to wage insurgency against my master. I needed to overthrow my oppressor — *fear* that had been crawling inside my head and burrowing itself deep into my subconscious.

I mumbled to Jason that I was going to jump off the five-meter platform. He replied but I didn't hear him. I took my first few steps up the stairs with confidence. As I progressed closer to the top, I felt my feet slowing down. My stomach was in knots. When I reached the top, I cautiously put one foot in front of the other as I neared the edge of the platform. I looked down at the pool below. My newfound courage and zest for adventure dwindled beneath me. All I saw was a fathomless pit of quandary. The sight of how high I was paralyzed my body as I imagined myself plunging below. I was scared stiff. My heart was racing as I shuddered standing on the ledge.

My mind kept conjuring up the panic of free-falling five meters down. I was petrified of taking the last step to let go. Frozen, I stared down at the knot of people watching me attempt the rite of passage to be one of the braves.

The lifeguard on duty folded his arms squarely across his barrel chest. Swimmers sitting by the pool flashed their curious smiles — waiting for a spectacle that had been built up far too long for anyone to care.

Who am I kidding! I can't jump! This is way too high, it ought to be illegal really... and the pool below is too deep! But wait, I can swim – even in deep pools... and maybe it's not that high, it's only five meters... Jason has done it... I can do it too... My mind raced as I took a trembling step.

Oh My God, I've been standing here for too long. I'm not going to die – I'll just plunge in the water and swim! I can swim! Once I jump, it will be over soon. I can't back down now! I'll be climbing down the tower of shame! I can't be on this ledge any longer! Just fucking jump, Emma! Jump! 1... 2... 3...

I backed away from the ledge. Heading to the stairs which led below, I trudged down the steps with a heavy heart. I have never felt more embarrassed, no matter how much I tried to convince myself that I did the *right thing*. I felt defeated for failing to free myself from my master — Fear, itself. I felt the sting of tears in my eyes. I was a coward. Always taking the easier path, too afraid to even give it a shot. I just wanted to run away and never come back to this place.

Jason met me at the foot of the stairs. He gazed at me with a sad-eyed smile. I turned my back against him and wiped my tears with the back of my hand..

"I think I'm just going to go home now. I'll see you around?" I put my head down and plodded away.

"Emma, do you want to try again?" Jason's voice was a husky whisper.

"I can't... I'm too afraid. I could never do it... I think I'm afraid of heights!" I looked away trying to hide the trace of shame in my face.

Jason locked eyes with me and flashed a crooked boyish grin.

"Yes you can, Emma... I know you really want to jump, or you would have not climbed up the tower and stood at the platform. If you go home now, you know deep in your heart that you will regret it."

His words rang true. I knew that I would feel worse rehashing this embarrassing moment if I went home without finishing what I started.

Jason's pep talk stuck with me like a hypnotic shaman mantra. He climbed up with me to the highest platform as I attempted to redeem myself from my previous diving meltdown. We got to the top, I took a couple of deep breaths before approaching the platform ledge.

A frail little boy, about seven years old, glanced at me as if anticipating that I would once again stand forever at the platform ledge — only to use the stairs back down.

"Can I go first?" He asked with freckled face, wet hair, and missing front tooth.

"Of course! Go for it!" I responded with enthusiasm trying to buy more time.

The boy quickly checked if the diving area was clear of the other swimmers. He stood at a distance back where he could build momentum. He then swiftly sprinted towards the ledge and jumped off in two seconds flat.

He did not waste any time psyching himself out, nor did he linger on the ledge surveying the depth of the pool or the height of the platform. He did not care at all about the people down below watching him. He was determined to jump when he climbed up and fully enjoyed the thrill of his daring stunt.

The little munchkin inspired me to just freakin' JUMP! As soon I checked that I would not be landing on another swimmer below, I did exactly what the boy did. No countdown from 1... 2... 3... I sprinted to the ledge and jumped off! I felt my stomach rose to my throat as my body was weightless in the open air. I plunged into the deep refreshing pool below and resurfaced with a gleam of triumph in my eyes. Shining faces welcomed me as I swam to the poolside.

Moments later, Jason back flipped from the tower and made a remarkable splash.

"I couldn't believe that I did it! I finally did it! I just went ahead and did what I climbed up to do!" I was on cloud nine! It was a different type of happiness — one that was fulfilling and made me feel alive!

"Yes, you did! That was amazing!" Jason looked proud of helping a friend take a chance. I thought of remembering that feeling of just jumping like my little munchkin hero in times of self-doubt. EMMA, JUST JUMP!

Later that day I was on my way home when I received a phone call. I answered, though I did not recognize the phone number.

"Hello?" I sounded cheeky due to my euphoric triumph from earlier.

"Hello, this is Marilyn Bray. May I speak with Emma?"

I was speechless. For the first time in my life, I heard the voice of the woman who gave me life. I have yearned for her no matter how much I denied it. I did not know what to say.

I was in a state of shock as I stood on the street with my mouth wide open, but not a sound came out. My head was spinning. Her voice faded in the background although I was holding the phone on my ear. I stared at a far distance of nowhere. When I relapsed, I heard her voice again:

"Hello? Hello!"

I must have zoned out for about a minute or more.

Another phone call was incoming, it was Laura.

"Shit!" I voiced out loud.

Okay... I got this. I'll put this call on hold and then answer Laura — tell her I'll call her back, then get back to my first call. Or maybe I should talk to my mother first... tell her I'll call her back...

I had a semi-functional plan until I pressed on the call answering options on the phone. I dropped a phone call.

"Hello?" said the voice from my phone.

"Hello..." Still partly dissociated, I responded but confused of whom I was speaking with.

"Hello! Let's have dinner tomorrow at my place!" It was Laura.

I accidentally hung up on my mother — on her very first call.

CHAPTER TEN

Mother Called

I agreed to meet up with Laura for dinner the next day. I didn't feel compelled to divulge the fact that I had just hung up on my estranged mother by accident. Mostly because I still couldn't believe it, and I'd prefer telling this to Laura in person. My mind was whirring around and around as Laura briefed me of our dinner plan. All I heard was, 'seven sharp', 'making carbonara', 'and bring white wine!'. I feigned listening intently and I heard myself say, "Can't wait! See you then. Bye!" while my mother's voice was still ticking away at the back of my mind.

My face was hot as I felt the blood rush to my ears. I kept having to close my eyes and take deep breaths, before I called my mother back. On the first ring, she answered in a soft, croaky voice. I introduced myself as Emma Bray and apologized for dropping her call. She graciously accepted my apology and asked how I was doing. My voice was dry as I uttered, *fine*' without reciprocating to ask her how she was. Suddenly, there was an excruciating silence between us.

"I'm so happy we finally found you, Emma..."

I sensed the crack in her voice. Feeling a pang of guilt for my cold response, I forced myself to reply with warm and friendly reverberation.

"It's nice to hear from you... I met Jackson, he's a fine gentleman." I said evasively.

"I can't wait to see you, Emma. We have a lot to talk about... Will you meet with me soon?" Her voice was small and brittle as she continued, "I've missed you so much..."

I was utterly dumbfounded to hear those words from my mother – the person who had abandoned me at birth and neglected me my entire life. I felt a swell of indignation. I wanted to condemn her in the most scathing tone I could muster but I couldn't get myself to do it. Instead, I swallowed hard and tried to sound unfazed.

"I'm going to be quite tied up studying for my final exams in the next few weeks. I don't think this is a good time. Maybe when it's all done..."

"That's fair, Emma... Maybe before Christmas?" Her voice was soft and hopeful.

"Okay, that could work..." I responded with an impassive voice.

My thoughts swirled in uncertain circles as we ended our call. All my life, there was a deep yearning inside me for a mother's love. But I learned to suppress this feeling as I grew tired of waiting for the day that she would come back for me. Now, after twenty-three years, she wanted to be in my life.

The next day I arrived at Laura's place accompanied with a bottle of *pinot grigio* to pair with her Italian pasta dish specialty. With classic reruns of Friends on TV as our ambient noise, I gave Laura a rundown of my family drama. She shared my shock of learning that my brother found me on the Internet via the viral video we took the day of the fundraising event. I told her that my mother became a dignified lawyer despite her history of deserting her own child, and that she had reached out to meet with me soon. I also told Laura about my animated anecdote of the unfortunate drop call, as I inadvertently blurted *'shit'* when my mother said *'hello'*.

"For what it's worth, you'll finally get the answer from her as to why she left and didn't come back... you know, to find closure..." Laura said with an outward veneer of calm.

"Yeah, I know you're right, that's all I'm really hoping for really... to finally get an explanation — no matter what it is..." I cleared my throat and swiftly swayed our conversation to a more cheerful topic. "Anyway, I also can't believe I'm graduating! All my courses will be finished by the end of this semester."

"Oh, right! I knew that! I'm so proud of you, Emma!"

"Well, it only took five years... and a massive student loan debt that'll enslave me for the next ten years... but I'm sure it'll be worth it." I replied with a wry look.

"Too bad there isn't a refund policy in case it doesn't work out!" Laura gave me a teasing grin. "When's your convocation so we could start looking for your dress! You need to wow the audience," Laura looked up wistfully.

"Well, good luck on us trying to outdo Andy. It'll be in Spring!

For the first time in a long while, I felt a lift in my spirits. I stood in the university hallway smiling broadly as everyone passed by. I watched the oscillating movements of students and listened intently to the clattering sound of conversations at lunch break. I felt a surge of excitement to start a new phase in my life. I was grinning from ear to ear as if all my fears had flown away like butterflies. I had dusted off my old self, and a new one was about to emerge.

A guy who saw me beaming in the corridor closed in on me. I gave him a quizzical look as he started flirting with me, convinced that I was staring and coming on to him. I was quite exalted since I thought my smile at that moment looked more like Jack Nicholson's creepy grin in '*The Shining*' than a foxy come-hither.

I strode forward hoping to fend off the young *Casanova* but he was already prancing next to me as if we're off somewhere together.

At last, I spotted Jason pacing down the hallway; his forehead furrowed in concentration while he fiddled with his phone. I tried to gesture awkwardly at him but he didn't notice my presence in the sea of students passing by.

"I almost didn't see you staring at me... then we finally locked eyes..." *Casanova* said while giving me a teasing grin.

My mind frantically spooled back. I *did lock eyes with him* with a beaming smile – all while feeling a warm glow of friendliness towards everyone in my moment of reverie! I may have led him to believe what's currently on his mind. My whole body stiffened.

"Uhm, actually I wasn't---" I said feeling a spasm of alarm.

"No need to be shy... this thing happens to me ALL THE TIME!" He gave me a wink as he pushed back his hair in a languorous way.

"Sorry, I really wasn't trying to—" I said in as I gave a gusty sigh.

"Why? You have a boyfriend?" He raised his eyebrows and simpered.

"Uhm, well..." All at once, I caught sight of Jason now almost at arm's length still looking at his phone.

"Baby! Babe! Boo! Bababoo!" I hollered at Jason to make it believable in front of *Casanova-slash-Gaston*. Jason didn't look, most probably because nobody has ever called him a silly pet name like *Bababoo* in real life. *I'm not sure if anyone does really.*

"Jason— Baby!!!" I yelled as I picked my way across the hallway, stumbling a little.

Jason finally looked over his shoulder and saw me grimaced in mock horror, while pointing my eyes to *Casanova* right behind me. I instantly clasped my arms tightly around Jason's arm and rested my head on his shoulder.

"This... My Boyfriend!" I squealed in broken English claiming Jason as my pretend partner as if declaring — *Me. Jane! He. Tarzan! while beating my chest.*

Casanova's eyes narrowed giving us a long, shrewd look. My throat gradually tightened but I didn't dare swallow. There was an infinitesimal pause in the air until I laughed out loud in my nerves.

I looked up, and Jason was already nodding conspiratorially. "Uh, yes, this... *is* my girlfriend!" He declared with a tiny smile at his lips while patting my head.

Jason's eyes fell on me. As I stared back at him in fascination, his cheeks were suddenly tickled pink. There's a spark of amusement in his eyes. He swallowed hard and touched my arm affectionately.

I couldn't help but feel a little flicker of pleasure as excitement bubbled away inside me. His arm crept around my body and slightly pulled me toward him.

Like magic, my body was light as a helium balloon tiptoeing delicately to be closer to Jason. I lifted my chin slowly until I was looking straight at him. I felt myself flush sensing the rise and fall of his deep breathing, prickling my skin.

"You guys! Get a room!" As though being wrenched from a beautiful dream, I heard a familiar voice interrupting my trance.

I opened my eyes and *Casanova* seemed to have been long gone.

Standing in the corner, I found Andy watching us with fondness. His inquisitive eyes ran over us. I jerked my hands away from Jason and hastily smoothed down my hair to get a hold of myself. I looked down and momentarily froze aghast. I had been incognizant of my surroundings in the height of sudden blissfulness.

I cleared my throat and both of our heads jerked up. His eyes met mine. I daintily tucked a lock of hair behind my ear and casually looked away. When I stared at him again, Jason was gazing at me wistfully. At once, I felt my face flooding with color. I gave a self-conscious laugh feeling utterly dumbfounded as I was dazed at the bashful smile that spread across Jason's face.

"Ughh, what am I trapped in some after school special?" Andy made a face as he walked over. I felt a rush of relief though as he broke the ice between Jason and me.

"Hey Andy, sorry, didn't see you there." I replied sheepishly.

"Oh I *bet* you didn't! So, you're finally *free*?" Andy giggled, bemused at seeing me nonplussed, knowing that he uttered something cryptic.

"Yeahhh... Just finished my last exam." I said trying to regain my composure.

"So am I—" Jason interjected as he beamed at me.

"Ah well, lucky bastards," Andy raised both his hands like a seasoned Vegas showgirl. "So, I can only assume you two are invited to the sickest party this New Year's Eve?"

Jason and I both shook our heads in unison.

"No?! Shame really... Oh well, you needn't beg... I've taken care of everything!"

"Here's your passes Emma, one for you and another for your plus one! Maybe you'll find somebody to kiss under the fireworks! Who knows? Anything can happen," Andy winked as he whipped out a couple of black and gold VIP tickets. The front cover read in big, bold letters: '*The Great Gatsby New Year's Eve Yacht Party*' with the sub-line: '*A night styled for the roaring twenties! Come dressed to impress!*'.

"Last year, I partied until the wee hours of the night going **GA-GA**... **SNOOP**in' around with **JEN** and **TOM**. **KANYE** believe it?" Added Andy looking amused of himself with a dreamy smile.

"Jeez Andy!" I exclaimed with a scoffing laugh "Sounds like a joke I'd make!"

"Oh my God you're right, I think I need a week-long cleanse! Anyway dear, awful jokes aside, you'll love it so you should attend, I bet it would be the best yacht party of the year!"

Jason and I locked eyes once more as Andy waited for our reply.

"So, do you want to be my plus one at the New Year's Eve Party?" I whispered, thoughtlessly fanning myself with my invite.

"Yes, definitely..." Jason muttered as his piercing baby blue eyes crinkled in a smile. I felt my heart flutter a bit as I stared back at him, all the while Andy giggled as he walked away.

CHAPTER ELEVEN

The Confrontation

I made a final attempt to check myself out in the mirror as I tried to ignore the flutters of apprehension in my stomach. Jackson had just called to let me know he'd be arriving soon to pick me up.

I wore a lean-fit black blazer over a white soft satin smocked blouse that was tucked in a pair of black straight-cut trousers. I'd put on some light neutral makeup and tied my hair up in a sleek high pony, letting my wispy bangs fall naturally on my face. I scanned myself from top to bottom for the final verdict. *Great. I look like I'm going for a job interview. Try-hard, much?*

Jackson arrived and parked outside my apartment. I hurried to put on my tried-and-true black leather loafers to finish off my '*business professional attire*'. Adrenaline was pumping through my body as I came out of the building. I suddenly felt a twinge of unease thinking of what was to come.

Maybe it's not too late for me to back out, I thought nervously, desperate to conjure up some silly excuse of why I wouldn't be able to make it.

I saw Jackson waiting in a white Porsche compact SUV with *'Macan S'* impressed on the trunk.

"Hey, Sis! Get in!" Jackson waved peering from the open window of his car.

The door closed with an expensive click as I sat inside the passenger seat. Jackson was all smiles wearing a crisp white chambray shirt and a navy blue cable knit sweater that hung over his shoulders. He looked like a dashing, cricket-playing, trust-fund baby casually heading out to some retro yacht party.

I tried to look calm while catching up with Jackson even though I kept feeling bursts of panic inside me. My hands were cold and clammy, and my heart was pounding in my chest. Without much thought I rolled down the window and tilted my head to the side taking in the passing breeze like a puppy going on a car ride.

Jackson hinted that we were nearing our mother's house right as we purred past some scenic hills, a lush golf course, and a ritzy country club — which was hidden from full view behind tall hedges. I started seeing fit, beautiful people going about their day, most of whom were walking their pure-bred French Bulldog, Yorkshire Terrier, or Bichon Frise. The neighborhood was filled with stunning historic houses ranging from Edwardian, Tudor, and Georgian style with well-manicured lawns. The quiet, cobblestone streets were lined with soaring trees.

We arrived at a well-kept two-story Tudor-style brick house with a quaint storybook appearance of a romantic English country home. There's a towering brick chimney and the windows were tall and massive with multiple panes. Jackson and I walked into the house through an embellished doorway bordered with contrasting stone against the brick walls.

He led me to the living room which was accented with dark wood ceiling beams and intricate wall paneling. The tables and bookshelves were made from oak and redwood, and accent decorations were mostly brass or glass crystal antiquities.

Across the room was a willowy looking woman with long black hair sitting on a French Provincial pink velvet gilded chair. She was wearing a blue nautical striped long sleeve shirt paired with a crisp white linen trousers and nude ballet flats. As I drew closer to her, I noticed that she had a freshly applied layer of make-up that gave her face some glow and definition.

She lifted the throw blanket off her lap and slowly stood up.

"Emma? Is that really you, my dear?" She said mildly as she took a light step and reached out both of her hands to cup my face.

Looking a bit sheepish, I said 'Hi' as naturally as possible. She gazed at me for a frozen minute, staring with a sympathetic face as tears abruptly welled around her eyes.

She reached out for a hug as I let her throw her arms around me. She held tight for what seemed like an eternity, as though making up for lost time. Her face lined with tears, she delicately stroked my hair just like my grandmother used to while putting me to bed.

For an instant, I wavered. Taking a deep breath, I tried to clamp my lips together and swallowed the lump in my throat. My heart sank. In one stroke, I wiped my eyes trying to regain control of myself.

I cleared my throat as I drew myself up. I felt like some gawky outsider as I took in the posh atmosphere of the drawing room. I noticed another tall middle-aged woman in the foyer speaking briefly with Jackson. I had no clue who she was, but from the way she was speaking it seemed like she was working for my mother, helping her around the house. Before I got a chance to ask about her, she waved goodbye to us and left.

As I took my seat, my mother offered me some tea and an array of scones, tartlets, butter tarts, crumpets, and madeleines of various flavors which were carefully laid out on the table.

Jackson left us alone so that we could talk in private. With bright eyes, she told me the story of how Jackson had found me on the Internet. She brought out a picture of me and my grandmother that was taken by our previous neighbor a few years ago. I listened politely as she narrated how she hired a private investigator to search for me all these years. I smiled weakly in return. After she finished, there was a prolonged silence that drowned the room and lingered an awkwardness between us. I felt a twinge of unease as I desperately looked around.

I darted my eyes over to a collection of pictures hanging on a gallery wall. I gazed from picture to picture: a candid photo of my young mother cradling a baby in the hospital bed right next to a man who was kissing her cheek; a scenic image of Jackson with my young mother and her husband merrily sailing on a boat. A panoramic image of their family vacation with the majestic Eiffel Tower in the background when Jackson was just about to hit puberty. A portrait of proud parents standing next to their prized only child who had just graduated high school. In a heartbeat, those images roused resentment and envy in me like some active volcano about to erupt.

"I know we have a lot to talk about... Where do I even begin..." She briefly paused. "Why don't I start— how's school going?" She touched my arm trying to make eye contact with me.

"Good..." I could not even look at her. "I'm graduating soon."

My voice was filled with apathy as I looked over at the taunting images while fiddling with tarts on my dessert plate.

"Oh, that's wonderful Emma! Jackson is graduating too, in the fall of next year!"

I felt a spasm of dismay. An avalanche of ire hit me with no warning.

I've waited twenty-three years for this day! Why the hell are we beating around the bush pretending that things are fine between us?

My head turned around as I eyed her with apprehension.

"When is your convocation, dear? Am I invited?" Her voice was teasing as she gave me a wry smile.

"Invited?' Why would *you* be?" I said with a scathing tone.

Her grin slowly faded. She looked completely taken aback.

My mother carefully got up and strode towards the high paneled windows. Then she stopped. Very slowly, she turned around, her face long and full of regret. "You probably hate me for leaving... I don't blame you... I should have come back and raised you—"

"Well how convenient for you, you finally found me when I no longer need you!" I said bitterly as I gave her a defiant look. I suddenly felt all the years of pent-up hurt rise up inside me.

She looked at me, utterly paralyzed. Her face lowered as she swallowed hard.

"Emma, please forgive—"

"*Forgive*? Is that the only reason you wanted to see me? You want my forgiveness? Tell me, *mother*, what kind of person abandons their own child?" I asked through clenched teeth, staring back at her with all the loathing of time.

Her face was frozen in horror. She put her hand into her mouth looking completely abashed with misty eyes.

"Save your tears for someone who cares. Do you have any idea of what it feels like to be discarded like trash?" I laid into her, I could not let this moment go.

"Why did you leave me? Why didn't you come back for me... Why couldn't you just... love me," I asked desperately, knowing no answer would make the pain stop. The torrent of words had come rushing out of my mouth like a waterfall as I broke down on the last one.

Taking a deep sob, I stood up with a heavy heart, turned my heel, and started to head off.

"Wait! Emma... I do love you..."

I stopped, flabbergasted into silence. I felt a thud in my chest which froze my body from running away.

"Emma, please, I was a selfish, terrible person... I am so sorry I left you... I am so, so sorry..." She cried desperately, slowly falling onto her knees.

A while after a whirlpool of emotions, we started talking about the elephant in the room. My mother regained her composure and jogged her memory.

"Charles— Jackson's dad..." She waved to his picture on the gallery wall. "When we were both in law school and engaged, we planned our future together from the get-go. He was smart, handsome, and ambitious... came from a wealthy family... the type of person who was obviously going places."

"How did you meet my dad?" I wanted her to let the cat out of the bag at all costs, so I swiftly interrupted her trip down memory lane with Charles.

"Oh, your dad, his name was David. A friend had introduced us at the mixer event I attended without Charles." She looked out the window with a thoughtful face. I followed her gaze as I held my breath.

"He was a young man from London, dressed impeccably without a hair out of place, a larger-than-life character, charismatic and smooth with words. He was the type of person who could sell ice to the Inuit," An air of melancholy surrounded her as she spoke.

"The truth is, I became infatuated with David after that night. Not long after we began an affair behind Charles' back. I fell head over heels for David and you were the fruit of that love. I called off the engagement with Charles and told him everything about the affair, and that I was pregnant with David's baby. It drove Charles up the wall, tore him to pieces. I was guilt-ridden and ashamed of what I had done to him, and I knew he didn't deserve it. David promised me that we'd start a life together in London. We planned on getting married and raising you there, Emma. It all seemed so beautiful and romantic at the time. But your father was a bit of a dark horse, I'm afraid, and there were a lot of things I didn't know about him." Her face grew tight, thinly veiling her heartache.

"He left for London to settle a few things before we'd live there. But when he hadn't returned after a few months, I began to worry. Even though I was pregnant I flew out to London all by myself. Not long after arriving, I found out that he had just married an English heiress. I could not believe it, I had to see him, had to hear it from him. I wasn't in my right mind when I decided to confront David at a private party. It wasn't my proudest moment, but I was desperate and torn up. I came down on him like a ton of bricks in front of their friends and family. He denied having a relationship with me and accused me of lying in front of a crowd. David kicked me out of the place, his face twisted in disgust at me as if to say, ' *Good Riddance!'* So to answer, yes, I know what it's like to be discarded like trash."

There was a grave expression on her face as she stopped. My mind was racing about all the accusations I had levelled at her moments ago, it made my stomach turn over. *Still, what happened to her doesn't justify what she did to me!* I couldn't help but think, even as my hardened heart softened.

"I hated him!" She cried, breaking the silence, as though the memory had struck a raw nerve. "When I gave birth to you, I had nothing to my name and no one to turn to. I had no choice but to come home to my parents and so I swallowed my pride and asked for their help in taking care of you. I was heartbroken, desperate, and miserable. I thought my life was over. I didn't have the time for both law school and to take care of my new-born child all on my own, so I left you mostly in the care of my parents."

"Not long after I had returned, Charles found out of my unfortunate fate. He eventually came to me to talk and reconcile. He still loved me and confessed that he wanted to marry me but made it clear that he wanted a fresh start. He wanted us to build our life together just as we planned it. He said he would forgive me and take me back, but... he felt that my baby... that you were a constant reminder of my infidelity and betrayal. He just couldn't accept it." Tears started rolling down my mother's cheeks as she clasped her blanket tightly to her chest.

"I thought that getting married to Charles was my only chance to start a new life. Your father didn't give a damn about either of us. Facing the chill wind of being a single mother and not be able to provide you with a good life finally made up my mind. So, when I came back to see you after six months, I told my parents that I was going to give you up for adoption. But mom and dad had already grown so attached to you, they loved you very much. They couldn't stand the thought of giving you away, and they were appalled that I would even think about giving you up for adoption to marry someone who doesn't want my own child. They offered to adopt you. Your grandparents and I had a long, bitter fight— things were said that haunt me to this day. And in the end, they decided to raise you and told me to never come back." Guilt and remorse were written all over my mother's face as she finished her tale.

I slumped down deeper in my chair and did my best to look unfazed. Something was nagging at me.

"Why didn't you go to their funeral?" I finally asked as my eyes narrowed.

"Charles and I moved to Switzerland right after law school. He found a business partner and started their first company there. By the time the years had gone on enough for old wounds to mend, I had lost all communication with mom and dad. I didn't know dad passed until years later. I tried to find you, Emma... I wished I had found you sooner... I missed your grandma's passing too... I was selfish and heartless... I chose the line of least resistance and it still brought me a life of grief." She swallowed hard. Her face was full of dread, her eyes staring out at some haunting apparition only she could see.

As angry as I had been, her words tugged at my heartstrings. She told me the truth, had laid bare her soul for me to see, and that's all I could have asked. In the end, all the shouting and holding in all the pain and bitterness made me feel no better. So, I let her tale wash over me and knew with time the hurt would slowly ebb away. I had found something that I had fiercely sought, without knowing I was seeking it. I had found closure.

"Thank you for telling me everything. I forgive you mom... and... I love you." With stiff knees, I lowered myself onto the floor and wrapped my arms around her. She gazed at me wistfully and threw her warm embrace over me like the protective cloak I had been longing for. For a still moment, I breathed a sigh of relief with a fond smile. As hard as it may seem, I meant every word I said.

Chapter Twelve

New Year's Eve Party

I stared at my reflection in the mirror with a slight note of triumph. I was wearing a tapered champagne-colored flapper dress embellished with beads and sequins and fringed in the hemline. I then jazzed up the *Roaring Twenties* look with a crystal headpiece, a white faux fur shawl and sparkly gold ankle-strap heels. I bought the entire ensemble from *Amazon* and got the package just a day before the party.

I fixed my hair up in a classic twenties wave updo, and dolled my face with wine colored lipstick, smoky eyes and a tad bit of light pink blush for a natural flushed cheeks glow.

Jason arrived at my apartment looking statuesque and dapper. He was wearing a slim-fit black tuxedo suit with shiny patent leather oxford shoes. Like cherry on top, his black bowtie and white pocket square completed his dashing and sophisticated appeal.

His hair was combed over on a side part, a nicely held pompadour. He looked like a strikingly handsome noble chap from the twenties.

"Hi! I guess I'm a bit early..." He said with a bewitching smile spread across his face.

I felt my heart lift. Flustered, I swallowed and then gave him a cheerful grin.

"No worries, come in for a minute. Andy should be here soon." I led him inside my apartment as I casually took a whiff of the fresh, woody, sensual cologne that trailed him. He smelled so irresistibly ravishing.

To ensure twelve months of good luck, I joked about eating twelve green grapes at the first stroke of midnight; devouring a grape on each chime — just like how the Spaniards would do it. Apparently all twelve pieces must be eaten at the final bell's toll. I told Jason that I would be going with *that* superstition in case I couldn't find someone to kiss me at midnight. Jason laughed, saying that drinking twelve ounces of wine would be less of a choking hazard. Or that I should just bang some bread on the walls just like how the Irish bring their good luck for the New Year. The thought of me whacking the only slice of stale bread I had left in my pantry on the wall made me burst into laughter.

As I led him inside my apartment, he gradually slowed his pace and turned to face me. Gazing at me for a long moment, he finally took a deep breath.

"I just wanna say... You look... breathtaking, Emma..."

His eyes met mine as my laughter melted away.

All at once, my heart started racing and my mind was blank. But a huge smile kept breaking through as I felt my stomach tighten.

"Thanks, Jason. You look incredible as well," I replied without a flicker, feeling my face flush pink.

There was a spark of amusement in his eyes.

Since I didn't even have a TV, video game consoles, karaoke machine, or whatever regular people own to entertain guests, I had to welcome him in my home, the old fashioned-way.

"Would you like to listen to some old records?" I said trying to sound casual.

"Sure, sounds wonderful."

I ran my fingers through my vinyl collection and all the while I felt his eyes on me. I glanced at him and caught his eye. I gazed down smiling as I picked up an *Etta James LP*.

Turning on my record player, I laid the album on the plate and put down the needle. With a tiny bit of crackle, the first song that played was '*A Sunday Kind of Love*'.

'I want a Sunday kind of love □

A love to last past Saturday night

And I'd like to know it's more than love at first sight

And I want a Sunday kind of love' □

The song played sweetly, with the warm hiss of an old record.

Oh my God, I've set the mood. I thought to myself, suddenly aware of what was happening. I didn't intentionally mean to play that song while my vanilla-scented candles were burning. The sweet romantic mood in my own home was enticing together with warm cozy Edison light bulbs dappling on Jason's dark blonde hair.

"Lovely song... A classic—" Jason nodded.

I nodded with an air of impartiality as if I was only appreciating the music for the sake of it and not noticing the mood that had just been set.

"Would you like something to drink?" I asked Jason, doing my best as a hostess.

"That would be great, thanks!" He replied back.

I went over to my tiny kitchen, three steps from my living room, and opened the fridge.

"Uhhm... Jason, would you like some—" I trailed off as I gazed inside, realizing that I had nothing good to offer. "Club... Soda...?" I cringed as I waited for his response. *Nobody drinks club soda on its own. Nobody. Except me.*

"Sounds good, thanks Emma."

Whew I thought as I poured cold club soda into a decent glass and served it to Jason.

He right away noticed the notebook he had gifted me sitting on my coffee table, with a pen tucked inside.

"How's the writing been so far? Found any inspiration for writing the next great novel?"

"Well, truth be told the pages are empty..." I gestured to the notebook with a little tilt of my head. "I've tried... But I just don't know how to start... I can't come up with anything good!" I felt embarrassed as I laid out all my dumb excuses.

"I get it but just write whatever comes to you. It doesn't have to be perfect... You just have to start. Eventually, it will open like floodgates." He had this sunny enthusiastic expression in his eyes.

"Yeah, I just don't know... I mean, who am I kidding? If I ever do write *one day*, who on Earth would read it? I'm just some nobody." I desperately stared at the floor, suddenly feeling defeated by my own insecurities.

"Well, I would read it, and I'm sure there are others who would as well. And if you ever decide to publish your work, I'm sure at the very worst we can convince Andy to buy enough copies to put you on the 'New York Times best seller's list" Jason said jokingly as he beamed at me.

"May I write a few words on the first page to get you started?" Jason asked as he took the pen and the notebook.

"Sure, go for it." I said without thinking much about it.

His eyes narrowed in concentration as he scribbled some words. He took a swig of his club soda, as though it were some fine Scotch.

He looked up and met my eyes once again. He grinned with a bashful smile and handed me the notebook.

I started reading as I mouthed the words in a murmur.

Every time I see your pretty face
Makes my heartbeat rise in pace
Memory of you is such bliss
A dream of your sweet lips' kiss

Whoa I thought, utterly bewildered. I blinked in total disbelief as I felt a surge of pleasure inside me. No one has ever made an acrostic love poem of my name before.

"Jason... Your words are... charming!"

I saw a flash of surprise in his eyes. My heart was pounding.

"How did you *just* come up with that?" I said, gaping at him.

"Words flow when inspiration is in front of me." He replied, without missing a beat.

I think he just professed his feelings. I just want to pounce on him and give him 'my sweet lips' kiss'...

I swallowed hard. My body started to feel hot. I slowly bent forward...

Then my phone rang.

Andy had just arrived outside my apartment to pick us up and take us all to the party.

Jason and I paused for what seemed like forever.

For that moment, I wanted to ditch *The Great Gatsby New Year's Eve Yacht party*. I didn't need to rapidly gorge twelve pieces of grapes nor bang bread on the walls to bring a year of good luck.

"Hello! Sorry I'm quite late! Are you coming out soon?" Andy's voice was shrill with excitement over the phone.

"Yeah... Uhm... We'll be right out." *Damn.*

As Jason and I walked out, a white, shiny Rolls Royce Phantom slowly pulled up right in front of us. Then a tall man stepped out of the driver's side wearing a sharp black suit; he looked like *Jason Statham* from *The Transporter*. He opened the rear-hinged door, which swung out in a dramatic flourish.

"C'mon lovebirds! Time to partayyy!" Andy shouted from the front passenger seat of the car. I knew exactly why he wanted to sit in front, right next to his attractive driver.

Andy was wearing a white suit-and-tie paired with brown oxford shoes, complete with a white fedora hat and a cane walking stick — just like a proper 1920's multimillionaire would.

Jason and I got inside the opulent rear passenger seat. The interior's plush white all leather seating, cashmere headlining, lambswool floor mats and LCD flat screen TVs made us feel like Hollywood superstars, or some big-time rappers.

Suddenly, the electric chauffeur-passenger privacy divider came down as Andy peered through, wide-eyed as though waiting to catch Jason and I on a full-on smooch session.

"Guys, could you be a dear and pop the champagne in the ice box? I'm quite parched! I glanced over and noticed there was a hardwood center console ice box. Opening it up, I saw the champagne and three flute glasses. Pouring drinks for all of us, Andy made a toast for love, sex and merry-making - all the while giving side-glances to our chauffer.

"Jason, Emma... Meet my favorite limo chauffeur, Mr. Stein. He's Norwegian! And hot!" Andy beamed as Mr. Stein gave him a suggestive nod and a smile.

"Mr. Stein is currently teaching me some Norwegian," Andy said with all seriousness, looking back at us as I made a face. "Oh come dear, I don't mean it that way. Well, don't get me wrong, *that's* happening too, but he's also actually teaching me some of his language. Well, mainly the curse words because you know! It's quite fascinating really," Andy carried on as we drove.

"So, Mr. Stein, what's the Norwegian word of the day today? Damn? Hell?..."

"*Dritt*, Master Andy, it means *shit* in my language," The driver said with all the seriousness of a Scandinavian gentleman.

"Oh well, how crass! I love it, ha!" Andy said with a laugh, clearly beaming at the fact that Mr. Stein referred to him as Master Andy in front of us. *Gawd Andy, I swear.* I thought half amused.

As we drove through the streets, a car suddenly swerved around the corner towards us. Mr. Stein narrowly avoided collision with it before I even had time to think. His reaction time was that of an impressive assassin. He saved all of us from harm.

And the half-million-dollar car he was driving. Jason and I were not wearing our seatbelts on.

Caught off guard, it took me a few seconds to realize that I was halted on top of Jason as champagne in my hand spilled onto the plush white leather seats.

I was on a crouching tiger pose hovering over Jason's body as though I was about to pounce on him. Our faces were only inches apart. And I was gawking at him like an apex predator. He gazed into my eyes with a charming smile. My mouth just opened... And then I closed it, as I became aware of what I was doing. I jerked away from Jason as I saw Mr. Stein glancing at us in his rearview mirror. My whole body was prickling. I was hot with embarrassment. I tried my best to look as if nothing out of the ordinary had just happened between us.

"Huh, well, what do we have here? Bit of an accident seems to have happened, I hope everyone is alright," Andy mocked us as I sat back down, getting off Jason.

"Oh, I didn't mean to fall on Jason," I said, feeling myself cringe with embarrassment.

"Oh I'm sure, that's definitely *not 'okse dritt'*. Oops, forgive me, *okse* means 'Bull' in Norwegian," Andy said with a smile to Mr. Stein.

Mr. Stein pulled over by the pier, right next to the docks that sprawled along the shoreline. We swiveled open the doors, rose out, while smoothing over our ensembles and exited the state-of-the-art modern-day luxury carriage.

There was a light breeze in the air, but it was nothing my *faux* fur wrap scarf couldn't withstand. And as if the god of the sky, rain, lightning and thunder had been in good spirits, the weather was calm and conducive for a lavish New Year's Eve celebration.

There was a luxurious yacht docked by the harbor shore boarding guests dressed to the nines like we were.

We set foot aboard the ritzy yacht. In an instant, our bodies were swaying with jazz dance music that was being played by the impeccably dressed orchestra - *Great Gatsby style*. The event was in full swing. In the blink of an eye, we were taken to the Jazz Age - the decade of prosperity and dissipation of flappers and old sports.

The yacht had three interior decks, a huge dance floor and an open-wide sky deck at the top. Strings of pearls and crystals hung from the ceiling, on the backs of chairs and off railings. There was a bountiful scrumptious buffet with appetizing entrées that we washed down with abundant champagne served around by gracious waiters. Our VIP tickets gave us exclusive access to the private lounge bars on the sky deck rubbing elbows with the vessel's captain and upper class society ala *Titanic*. I felt like the poor third-class *Jack Dawson* who boarded the ship after winning a lucky game of poker. Thank God we were no near the North Atlantic Ocean, or I would have doubted my luck.

Ladies donned shimmering silk gowns adorned with sequins, crystals, fringes and fur with sparkling shades of gold, topaz or jade. Gentlemen looked dazzling in tuxedos and formal suits complete with bow ties, pocket squares or hats. Although there were a few who toned down the opulence, most were resplendent. The sky deck was the best vantage point for the spectacular fireworks to be had at midnight, so we hung around there as the new year approached.

Andy stood right next to Jason and me as we nibbled on hors d' oeuvres and sipped fizzing champagnes.

"Oh God," Andy gaped. "My frenemy is heading our way, three o'clock. Now don't be intimidated," Andy met my gaze square on. "And no matter what Emma, never, ever admit that you got your dress from Amazon, or she'll rip out your soul!"

"What? How did you—" I said through a mouthful of shrimp. *Classy.*

"Oh honey, I know..." Andy interrupted, giving me a raised eyebrow look.

"There you are! Andy! I've been looking all over for you my dear!"

A tall, slender, elegant-looking lady with porcelain skin, onyx black hair, crimson lips and beautiful dark eyes approached us.

"*Feng!* My God, it's been *too* long! Since Paris Fashion Week, I believe." Andy blurted as they air-kissed each other's cheeks on both sides without actually touching.

"Missed you." She eyed him as she mildly ran her hand on the fabric of his sleeves. "Looking rather charming in a Tom Ford suit. And the cane — that added *pizzazz*!" She nodded as though giving Andy her seal of approval.

"Only the best, my love! But look at you! So fantabulous in a Limited Edition Miu Miu flapper gown... embellished with Swarovski crystals, of course. Such a *piece de resistance*!"

Why do these people talk like this? I gaped at them as I watched in total disbelief.

Suddenly, two other hoity-toity ladies dressed in 1920s bedazzled perfection, one in blue and the other in red, joined the charade like *Regina George's* sidekicks from *Mean Girls*. All at once, they whispered cunningly to Feng's ear as I tried to read the muted expression on her face. They were giggling and nudging one another as they glared at the pretty young blonde girl flirting with a gentleman, who I later found out was Feng's brother.

"The nerve..." The girl in blue sniggered.

"She's such a gold-digger!" Scoffed the one in red.

"She admitted it! I caught her off guard... She's wearing a dress from *Forever 21*! I mean, can you even imagine?" She turned to Feng in horror. "She didn't even try!"

I felt a stab of shock. *Yes, the 'pretty blonde' girl's dress may be a little bit too tight fitting and above the acceptable hemline. But,* I thought, *all in all, she looked very lovely in her black fringe halter dress. Why should it matter if it was from Forever 21? I mean I got my dress from Amazon for forty-five bucks... I have Forever 21 dresses at home, and most of my clothes are even from Thrift Shops. That was a bit mean.*

The pretty blonde walked towards us as she spoke a friendly "Hi, Feng!" with a shy wave.

Feng met her eyes with a little smirk and then gave her a scathing *up and down look*. She turned to her sidekicks as if the pretty blonde was invisible.

The poor girl was understandably beyond mortified. Her cheeks flamed crimson as she hurried to leave before she could stop herself from sobbing shrilly.

The two girls in red and blue, along with Feng turned to us with a mocking laugh.

I was wide-eyed, barely able to stop myself from clasping a hand over my mouth. *That was harsh.* She was a mean *Queen Biatch* and I suddenly didn't like her. Yes, she's beautiful and probably the heiress to some multimillion-dollar empire but I didn't care, I just knew I didn't want to be her friend. Nor her frenemy for that matter.

She swiveled her head toward Jason and leaned forward confidently. She smiled broadly at him and introduced herself.

"Feng Yan..." She extended her delicate hand to Jason expecting it to be kissed. She seemed genuinely fascinated by him, and didn't even look at me. As her delicate hand was extended, she moistened her lips with her tongue. I couldn't help but feel off as she was obviously flirting with my date.

Jason looked taken aback but obliged anyway to the chivalrous act of hand kissing like an old-fashioned gentleman. He then uttered, "Jason Sherman..."

"Delighted to meet you, Mr. Sherman... Looking quite dashing tonight!" Feng locked eyes with Jason as she gave a tinkling laugh. She ran her fingers through her neck, bit her lower lip, and batted her eyelashes while she flustered.

What the heck is this, 'Pride and Prejudice'? Hand kissing and 'Delighted to meet you'? I felt a pang of jealousy. *Jason is supposed to want my sweet lips' kiss... he said so in his poem!* I felt like I randomly landed in the middle of some weird dream. *I can't believe Feng's snatching my date right before my eyes.*

"Oh, Feng! Forgive me for not introducing them! This is Emma, Jason's date." Andy blurted out.

"Hmm, is that so?" Feng turned to face me and tilted her head on one side with narrowing eyes as if sizing up her competition.

"Yes, that's quite right— I'm Emma's New Year's Eve date" Jason said abruptly as he wrapped his hand around my shoulder.

"I see, well, nice dress, Anna... Who are you wearing tonight?" She asked, looking stricken. I'm pretty sure she deliberately misspoke my name.

Oh God. Am I going to be the next victim of this fabulous but nasty Asian Regina George?

I apprehensively raised my head and started to speak. "It's from Ama---" I darted my eyes over to Andy whose eyes were bulging in horror while miming the word *'No!'* as though he was going to suffer a heart attack if I said 'Amazon'.

"Uh, it's an up and coming designer..." I trailed off evasively.

"Oh really... from where?" Asked Feng incredulously.

"Nor... Norway!" I replied in a strangled voice.

"Norway? What's the name of the brand?" Her brow crumpled.

I stood there staring, with a bewildered look on my face. All eyes swiveled toward me, but my mind was blank.

"Oh, it's indie... kinda like *Banksy* but for fashion design" I said coolly as I swallowed.

"Oh? What's it called? I'm going to Oslo next week! I wouldn't mind checking out this up and coming *designer.*" Her dismissive eyes ran over me.

"It's called..." I closed my eyes and cast my mind back. Then, as if a light bulb switched on inside me, "*Dritt!*" I exclaimed with a whoosh of relief.

Andy and Jason both had their eyes wide open trying to suppress their laughter.

"*Dritt?*" Feng blurted out loud.

"Yes... *Dritt!* And you know what? I think you're going to *love* it!" I gave a relaxed smile, took a sip of champagne and sauntered off anchored in Jason's arms.

Jason and I luxuriated in the temperature controlled glass-covered sky deck with stunning 360 view of the city skyline and open water. Champagne and hors d'oeuvres were everywhere and the jazz band music was enchanting. Andy had disappeared after wooing a hot Italian yacht crew member. He gave us strict instructions not to interrupt his tryst under any circumstances.

A few minutes before the New Year's Eve countdown, a beaming waiter rushed to Jason and me with a plate of green grapes, a couple of French baguettes, and two glasses of champagne. Jason winked at me as I realized he had arranged for all this sometime during the party.

"How did you get all of these together so fast?" I fiddled with the grapes in amusement and thoughtlessly placed one in my mouth munching on it before midnight.

"I found a friend who could pull some strings..." Jason gave me a teasing grin.

"Just a minute more..." He whispered softly raising my chin as though jogging my memory of the Spanish superstition.

On the spur of the moment, without thinking, I touched his lips with my fingers and offered to put a grape in his mouth. He nodded, as I gazed deeply into the sea of his eyes. His mouth parted, giving way to the sweet, succulent fruit of intoxication.

"Shouldn't we be eating the grapes at the strike of midnight?" Jason murmured as he swallowed the grape.

"There are other New Year's superstitions..." I insinuated before I could stop myself.

Enraptured in a trance, the reverberation of excitement within the air was infectious, yet for us it was only subliminal. The most awaited moment was only a few seconds away.

"Four... Three... Two... One! Happy New Year!" The yacht was overflowing with resounding laughter, giggles and cheers from gabbling spectators.

For an infinitesimal moment, we both looked up in fascination at the fireworks that shot up into the sky before it exploded into cascading sparks like a glittering silver shower. Fizzing, effervescent gold pinpricks in Ferris wheel shapes scattered across the sky, taking off in all directions.

Jason looked at me with urgent, aroused eyes. I swallowed in excitement as my fingers fell gingerly down his chest. My ribcage was rising and falling. I looked down feeling dizzy with exhilaration, trying to get a hold of myself. When I looked up again, his gaze was fixed on mine. I felt a rush of surprise, with butterflies in my stomach lifting me from the inside; I could just float up into the sky. As though in a mystical cloud of bewilderment, the clattering frenzy around us seemed to have fizzled out into a quiet, ambient sound.

He caressed my face and pulled me effortlessly towards him. Spellbound, I felt myself drifting on cloud nine. As I drew closer to Jason, his warm body evoked a ripple of sensation inside me. His masculine musky scent elated my senses into another level of euphoria. Without restraint, he slowly bent forward whilst my eyes closed in anticipation.

I felt our lips touch for the first time.

His mouth opened mine and softly sucked gently on my lower lip. He then teased my excitement with a flourish of his tongue. The fireworks became a supernova.

As if freediving into the abyss, our lip-locking reverie was unrelenting. I felt him run his fingers through the back of my hair and pull it back with a deep hunger. A surge of erotic pleasure rushed down my spine. I kept kissing him, running my hands up his broad shoulders as I found my arms settling around his neck. He held me by the waist and a jolt of lightning struck my core. His soft, supple lips was a fountain of ecstasy.

Suddenly thoughts of Mark that was once submerged in the deepest trench of my subconsciousness started bubbling to the surface. I felt a pang of guilt from my budding fling. But I reasoned against my own moral sense that Mark was no longer my lover; that we had decided it was best to separate and *maybe* revisit our lives down the road. As much as I cared for Mark, we made no promises and I was not beholden to him, nor him to me. Jason's blissful kiss was passionate and thoughtful. My brain suddenly recognized that I was doing something right. I wished that moment lasted for an eternity.

As we pulled away slightly, we stared at each other in fascination.

He blinked in seeming disbelief and then fixed me with an intense gaze. I could still feel his skin on mine. He suddenly wrapped his arms around me and clasped me tight against his chest. I finally raised my head up and looked at him. I felt my cheeks tickled bright pink. He held my hand and locked his fingers with mine as we looked over at the crystal view of the night sky, the last of the fireworks booming up above.

I felt like we were at the top of the world as I took in the breathtaking vista. Burning colors of the sky's festivity were etched into my mind as the final celestial rays catapulted up from below, and traced spiraling glimmer of light through the darkness.

This drew out long *"oooohhs"* and *"aaaahhhs"* from the surrounding crowd as they marveled at the spectacle of the night. Luminous gamut of colored sparks danced and flickered non-stop colliding into one another like a kaleidoscopic finale.

At last, applause rippled around as the last clusters of golden starbursts vanished into the night sky.

Just before the night ended, Jason and I started gobbling down one grape at a time as we frolicked feeding each other with a mouthful of fruit. After the twelfth grape, we moved on to whacking the baguettes against the nearest wall surface of the sky deck like a couple of zany buffoons. We were having the best time of our lives.

"So, are you two ready for the *real* Gatsby party?" Andy said as he sprung out of nowhere, looking slightly disheveled from his exhilarating rendezvous.

"What do you mean the *real* Gatsby party?" Jason and I looked at each other in puzzlement as Andy gave us this devilish grin.

Chapter Thirteen

Bunker Mansion

Jason, Andy and I tripped happily down the stairs from the sky deck as the yacht sailed back to the pier. When we got back, Mr. Stein was waiting for us nearby.

"Happy New Year, Mr. Stein!" Said Andy with wide eyes and a knowing smile as he got into the car.

"Same to you, Master Andy. You seem to have had a jazzy time!" Mr. Stein smiled at Andy and studied his face for a few moments.

"A little bit..." Andy looked flushed and shiny. "Anyway, the night's still young, and so we shall head off to Gatsby's!" Andy exclaimed in a stagy, melodramatic voice.

"As you wish, Master Andy." Mr. Stein held the car's gear knob and drove off away from the pier smoothly.

I wonder how much Andy's paying him per hour to repeat saying Master Andy like Bruce Wayne's loyal butler. I wondered as we drove back onto the main roads.

Jason slowly delved his fingers into mine as I rested my head on his broad shoulders, taking in his bewitching scent.

Andy didn't want to give us any hint of where the party was going to be after our ritzy New Year's Eve bash on the luxury yacht. My mind was buzzing with different possible venues for Gatsby's *real* party.

It must be some kind of a colossal mansion by the bay, or a grandiose neo-renaissance style hotel, or a penthouse suite somewhere glitzy. It could be on a plane.. a train... At this point, the sky's the limit! I thought as I raced over all the possibilities.

After a while, I looked out the window and saw a pawn-shop and a payday loan place right next to each other. A block away, there was an establishment called *Billy's Bubble Car Wash* with a huge red sign around it that read – 'Laundromat. Pizza. Convenience Store. Chicken. Car Wash. Ice. ATM Machine'. A one-stop-shop that catered to all its neighborhood necessities.

Next was a fast-food shack called *KFC* – **Kebab-Fries-Chicken** with a red, gaudy neon sign. All the while we passed shops and corner stores with barred windows and front doors. To be honest, the neighborhood looked a bit rough and tumbled. Normally I wouldn't be concerned, having grown up in similar areas myself, it wasn't something out of the ordinary for me. However, what did concern me was we were travelling in a half million-dollar car with *Andy* — a fellow whose shoelaces probably cost more than my entire wardrobe.

Mr. Stein took a sharp turn down a dark, back alley where most of the streetlights were burnt out. He then pulled up next to a huge dumpster.

"Okay, we're here! Are you guys ready for *the best party of your life*!?" Andy sounded like a club hype man, smiling proudly.

Feeling a tad nervous I whispered, "Ummm... Where?"

"Welcome to *haut monde*!" Andy sounded like a deluded cult loyalist as he made sweeping gestures with his arms.

"Uh-huh, and that means?" I murmured as I stared at him incredulously.

"Why, *High Society* dear! Oh, just trust me!" Andy waved as he could see my skepticism grow.

There was a bewildered silence as I swallowed hard and peered out of the window, frantically looking left and right. There was no one else in sight who was dressed up like we were.

The only security I was holding on to was Mr. Stein's *"specific set of skills"* in case somebody decided to jack us.

As they rightfully should. We're in a dark back alley. At one o'clock in the morning. Aboard a swanky car. With a multi-millionaire heir as their target kidnappee. I mean, we're just asking for it. Begging somebody, anybody — to take advantage of the situation. Gawd at the very least this will teach him! I thought as I stepped out of the car, peering around.

Andy, Jason and I walked about thirty feet away from the car as Mr. Stein carefully watched us get in front of a huge rusty steel door lit by a single, flickering incandescent light bulb. The metal door had an enormous rectangular metal plate and a bronzed lion's head knocker in the middle. I turned on my heel and took a few steps away to read the sign above.

When I looked up, the sign read: **Jensen Janitorial Supply Co.**

Right. 'Haut monde'! He said... 'just trust me' He said...

I shot Jason a look as I gestured my head toward the farcical sign.

"Are you sure we're in front of the right door?" My voice sounded reluctant.

"A hundred and ten per cent!" Andy said without looking at me.

He pounded the lion's head door knocker three times as it made frightening loud noises.

The rectangular metal plate slid open at full tilt with an echoing ping. A man peered through the most ridiculous gigantic peephole revealing both of his dilated eyes strung with visible bags underneath.

"We're closed." The man peered at Andy as his eyes narrowed.

"I'm here to see the man in the green hat." Andy uttered in a low voice.

"I'm sorry sir, but *that ship has sailed*." The man behind the steel door was quite posh sounding.

Andy's face blanched in shock. He then jerked his chin up looking offended.

Jason and I exchanged glances as we stood behind my dear friend who just wanted to show us '*the best party of our lives*'. Whatever may be behind that door. I felt a surge of sympathy for Andy. That was the very first time I've ever witnessed him not get his way.

As I was about to put my hand on Andy's shoulder to comfort him, he drew himself up and said with utmost pride and conviction:

"MY NAME IS ANDREW CORBIN HAWTHORNE, *THE THIRD*."

Like lightning, we heard sounds of the latched metal door magically unlocking from the inside as though Andy's name was the modern '*Open Sesame!*'

"My sincerest apologies, Mr. Hawthorne... I was not informed you were to be arriving. Welcome to Gatsby's! And, Happy New Year, Sir." A man in a sharp silk grey suit who looked exactly like Ray Liotta in *Goodfellas* gestured his hand to invite us in.

The door slammed shut with a clang behind us after we stepped inside.

"It's quite alright. It was just a little chilly outside, that's all. Thank you for enforcing a strict security of the facility." Andy smiled thoughtfully at the doorman.

"Please make yourself at home, Mr. Hawthorne." He nodded with a polite incline of his head.

Looking around, I was not surprised to see a normal looking janitorial supply store. Fluorescent lights illuminated the isles of bathroom care, floor care, paper products, dispensers, odor control. There's Mr. Clean, Windex, and Pledge products. It all checked out. *Jensen Janitorial Supply Co.* was legit. There were even a couple of cash registers and a Customer Service corner.

Except for the four sharply suited gentlemen who were guarding the store at that hour, everything about the place seemed like some hum-drum janitorial supply store. And it didn't seem logical to see them all suited up just to guard the cleaning merchandise.

We followed Andy as he strode directly to the back of the store. No one stopped us as we ignored the *'Employees Only'* sign above the door. Andy swerved to a corner hallway and opened another door that led to a metal spiral staircase that was dimly lit.

As we descended down the stairs, I felt myself getting exhausted and dizzy from the endless steps going straight down to God knows where.

"Andy, I don't feel well going down these stairs... I might just go back up," I said feeling a bit sick as I slowed down trying to regain my balance.

"I'm sorry you're feeling ill Emma, we're almost there, just a few steps more. I can almost see the *door.*" Andy and I were breathing hard while Jason didn't express any sign of fatigue.

"What *door*? There's *another* door?" I said in disbelief.

"Don't worry, we won't be getting out the way we came in!" He sounded encouraging.

"Where exactly is this party? The ninth layer of hell?" I half joked as Andy and Jason both chuckled.

We finally reached the bottom of the staircase as we all sighed in relief. It was dim all around with just a few lightbulbs from a distance. My optimism was slowly dying away. I came down for a good time, not to feel as though I was trapped underground in some crypto-conspiracist's bomb shelter.

Right next to the bottom of the staircase was a tiny office with a brass plate sign that read, **'A.C.H.'** The door was opened for Andy as he placed his thumb fingerprint on a biometric lock that cleared his security check. Inside the office were stacks of old newspapers and books on the floor and table. He closed the door shut behind us and walked towards another door lined with ten doorknobs.

Seriously, this is a bit much for a party.

Jason and I stood behind Andy in silent frustration. *I guess he just wants us to be a part of his world. And I'll be there for him. Wherever that may be.*

Andy gripped the fifth doorknob from the top.

Jason and I were wide-eyed in anticipation. Andy shot us a look of excitement as if to say — *'It's gonna blow your minds!'*

Then Andy faced the door, turning the knob very slowly when - as if taken by a gust of wind, he swung the door open.

We took a few steps in and suddenly, we were in the world of *haut monde* - High Society indeed.

"Here we are!" Andy spread his arms in the air as though welcoming a fresh breeze of triumph.

Our jaws were hanging in disbelief.

It was like we were taken to the most opulent hidden world. We were standing inside a *neo-baroque* ballroom with a grand staircase. The mesmerizing underground mansion was illuminated by soft, whimsical lights from crystal chandeliers hanging above. Wall-to-wall gold-framed mirrors reflected the beauty and grandiosity of the place.

We were greeted by *'The Master of Ceremonies'* who sported a jet-black tailcoat, a black top hat over his head and a dark varnished cane in his hand.

"Mr. Hawthorne! You've graced us with your presence!" His smile was welcoming as Andy introduced Jason and me as his guests for the night.

The guests inside were all dressed to kill as the servers walked around with fine cocktails, champagne, and scotch. There was a widespread frisson about the room.

Gigantic white ostrich feathers, rose gold velvet draperies and luxe tufted furniture decorated every corner of the place. A live jazz band entertained the ballroom with aerial acrobats in flapper costumes hanging from the gargantuan chandeliers that hung across the towering ceilings.

As though the grand marble staircase was not enough, there were brass birdcage elevators with elaborate design trimmings. Gatsby's iconic yellow Rolls Royce vintage ride was parked in the middle of the ballroom like a centerpiece.

The ambient dim lighting sparked a glamorous, romantic mood. There were private and intimate tables by the balcony for those who wanted a fancy restaurant-style dining with multiple courses served by dedicated servers. Andy, Jason and I strode straight to a table that had a good view of the party.

I ordered a Manhattan, Andy had an *Old Fashioned* cocktail, while Jason had a glass of *Glenfiddich* whiskey. We feasted on a four-course French meal that we barely finished and luxuriated on the beauty of the ambience. It was as though we were in *Alice's magical wonderland.*

"Andy, I just want to say thank you for taking me and Jason to the yacht party and here... whatever, wherever this is..." I said happily as I took a sip of my drink.

"To Andy!" Jason raised his Scotch. "A beautiful man, inside and out!" He finished his toast with a charismatic wink. Andy raised his glass in acknowledgement of our compliments.

"You guys! I told you, I'd bring you to *haut monde*!" His face lit up as though he finally satisfied our wildest dreams.

"Andy, I have to ask, what is this place? And why is it in such a shabby neighborhood? And why so much secrecy?" I poured out a fountain of questions as I gave Andy a curious look.

"Okay, alright! I'll confess..." Andy was teasing me as he took his time sipping his drink while I stared, waiting for answers.

"This place is a decommissioned military bunker that my family bought a long time ago and turned it into a luxurious shelter. What you're seeing right now is just a part of the many amenities hidden from plain sight. My grandfather and his business partners bought hundreds of bunkers and silos that were abandoned by governments in different countries after the

war ended and turned them into *'luxury doomsday bunkers'.*
You know, just in case of global pandemic, asteroids, zombies,
World War III... whatever!" Andy was surging with pleasure
gazing at our reaction as he sipped his drink.

"Wow, that's crazy! Well, I guess I know where to go in case
of an apocalypse!" I declared with genuine fascination written
all over my face.

"Oh honey, you'll be the first one I tell!" Andy gave me a
hopeful look and then turning over to Jason "Actually, given
how Jason looks in a tuxedo, maybe you'll be second Emma!"

Shaking my head, I shot Andy a series of questions about
their *'luxury doomsday bunker business'.*

"Whatever! Okay, so now let's say someone would be interested in buying one of your finished luxury bunkers, how much
for a one bedroom, one bath?" I asked trying to sound casual.

"Oh I have no idea, but honestly if you have to *ask...*" Andy
bantered with a smirk, then raised his eyebrows suggesting that
it's out of my tax bracket.

"What other facilities are available for bunker owners?"
Chimed in Jason as though a prospect buyer.

"Let's see, there's five-star restaurants, opera houses, coffee
shops, pools, game areas, luxury boutiques, hydroponic gardens, spas, gyms.... Everything really... but I just mentioned the
essentials!" Andy answered on impulse.

"Did all these people come through the *Jensen Janitorial Supply* store?" I asked glancing around the room filled with people.

"No, that portal was just for the *Ultra VIP*. It was the only
way we could get in after the cut off time at midnight. The club
members have different passages." Andy said with all seriousness as if he were some travel guide.

"Most are discrete trap doors in public places – like a washing
machine at a laundromat, a fridge inside a meat shop, a public
restroom at the subway station... they're where you would least
expect them!" Andy looked so animated as he described how
they all work.

"Okay, last question – Who's the man in the green hat?" I eyed Andy suspiciously.

"Oh dear, that's the password to get in. It changes though, so don't try to use it without me or you might have to face severe consequences!" He folded his arms and gave me a shrewd look.

"Wow, seems harsh, like what kind of harsh punishment?" I asked staring at him intently.

"Oh, the harshest of all — Public humiliation! Mr. Thatcher, the doorman, will give you *such* a tongue lashing and not the good kind, believe me!" Andy said with a slight smirk.

"Oh, sounds dreadful!" I said laughing at the thought that Andy really considered being told 'you couldn't come in' was a "severe" punishment.

Andy paused for a moment then continued, "But the real *man in the green hat* refers to a man who used to personally deliver illegal booze to Congress and the Senate during *Prohibition* times. Such a ballsy bastard!" Andy sniggered.

Out of the blue, a thought bolted to Andy's mind.

He blurted out, "Oh, Emma! I almost forgot I *must* say hi to a few people here tonight! I'll be right back, as long as Mr. Mars doesn't talk my ear off!"

Andy excused himself and strode off. *He couldn't possibly mean that Mars, could he?* I wondered looking around for the singer sensation.

I glanced around for a bit but I could see no one I knew or recognized — famous or otherwise. I looked back to Jason who was smiling at me. I smiled back at him as he held my gaze for a moment. An idea just crystallized in my mind.

"Are you up for a fun game of rapid-fire question and answer?" I exclaimed like an *Emmy* award-winning game show host.

"Sounds great! Fire away!" Jason blurted out without a flicker as he took a sip of whisky.

"Okay, let's do three rounds! And no repeating of questions." I smiled and felt a surge of excitement.

"I'll ask first…" Jason said, and met my eyes with a little snicker. "What's your go-to joke?"

"Well, what sounds like a sneeze and is made out of leather?" I paused for my punch line…

"*A shoe*!" A hysterical giggle rose inside me. Jason was shaking his head, trying to suppress a smile.

"Whatever, it's a classic! Okay, my turn!" I said with a grimace. "What's the silliest thing you're passionate about?"

"Skydiving." He gave a bashful smile then proceeded to ask me a question right away before I could respond. "What's the *funniest* picture you've taken today?" His zestful voice was infectious.

I grabbed my phone and scrolled through my saved photos… I sent him a picture of us posing cross-eyed with a mouthful of grapes, holding French baguettes, taken just a few hours before. He glanced at the picture then instantly dissolved into hysterical laughter.

"Okay, what's the *best* photo you've taken today?" I asked half laughing.

He went through his phone and sent me a picture of us from the sky deck of the yacht standing close to each other. His arm was around me looking down at my face and I was gazing up at him. It was a candid photo beaming with happiness. If it weren't us, I would have thought it was an advertisement for a dating site.

I felt myself color a bit, so I took a sip of my drink and swallowed hard. My heart was pounding. I felt an explosion of delight. *The best picture in his phone is a picture of us together.*

"Okay, last question…" I cleared my throat and tried not to gabble. "What's the funniest movie quote you know?"

Jason looked up in the sky for a quick moment as though browsing through years of collected movie quotes saved in his long-term memory.

"Here's a classic --- Blues Brothers, 1980… Dan Aykroyd and John Belushi were trying to make it to their gig on time:

Dan Aykroyd: *'It's 106 miles to Chicago... we got a full tank of gas... half a pack of cigarettes... it's dark, and we're wearing sunglasses.*

John Belushi: *Hit It!"*

I laughed thinking fondly back on those old movies.

Jason and I played a staring contest for a good minute until I couldn't help it anymore. I smiled, looked away and burst out laughing. He held his gaze at me and shot me a dazzling smile. He seemed to be genuinely fascinated staring at my funny face.

"Do you want to wander around and maybe look for *Mr. Mars*?" Jason murmured.

"Mr. Mars? Ohhh... right. Well, that's an offer I couldn't refuse..." I nodded, feeling a bit chastened.

Jason and I slowly made our way to the farthest and most dim part of the foyer. Climbing a beautiful set of spiral stairs, we found ourselves up above, on one of the balconies. It was a quiet spot away from the crowd, but it overlooked the guests in the ballroom below. Everyone was still partying the night out — dancing, drinking, flirting...

All of a sudden, the music mellowed. I heard someone started playing the grand piano but I couldn't get myself to take my eyes off Jason. A familiar song permeated with romance in the air.

'Come away with me in the night ☐

Come away with me

And I will write you a song' ☐

It was stunning to hear, and it could have been the wonderful Norah Jones herself by the sound of the singer's voice. I felt a renewed surge of exhilaration as Jason locked eyes with me.

"I really love this song..." I whispered.

"May I have this dance?" Jason extended his left hand with his palm up. His face broke into a charming smile.

I looked around and found no one else near us in our tiny private nook up on the balcony.

"Sure..." I said quietly as my face turned bright pink.

Jason rested his hands gently at my waist and I reached up both of my arms slowly around his neck. Our heads moved toward each other. He smelled heavenly. I was drawn to his warmth and magnetism like a bewitched willing subject under a hypnotic state. We were trading breaths as we danced, my head resting on his chest. I breathed out, he would breathe in. I was entranced feeling his warm breath tickle down my skin.

I looked back up at him, my lips parted and so was his... our mouths were barely touching. Bit by bit, I closed my eyes like a serene sunset after a beautiful summer day. Patiently waiting to suck the sweet nectar from his mouth. I felt his body tense near mine, his hands sliding down my backside and lifting my dress. *I can't believe this!* I felt my mind racing as we kissed, my hands running down his chest and stomach, stopping at his belt. *Am I really going to make love to him? But where? I couldn't up here, it's way too open and such an "Andy" thing to do! God, do I want him though and I can tell he wants me.* We kept kissing as his hands gripped me hard from behind, as if he needed to take me right then and there.

Suddenly, I heard the music changed and I stopped as though wrenched out of some fairytale. The song *Blue Moon* began playing from the party below, the song that Mark and I shared. I pulled away from Jason on impulse and looked down. I saw a man who resembled Mark passing by which drove a sudden twinge of guilt inside me.

I must be drunk. Am I hallucinating? How much champagne and Manhattan cocktails did I have tonight? No, Mark is not here, he can't be. He needs a password to get in... It's just my mind playing tricks on me.

Why am I feeling guilty though? We're not together anymore. But — it's only been a couple of months and I still think about him...

I think... I think I still love him.

But I'm so drawn to Jason. And I have desires... urges that he can fulfill. I really like him. It's going to be our own little New

Year's Eve fling. Yes, I'm a little buzzed but I know exactly what I'm doing. I am in the right mind to get what I want. And I want Jason tonight.

"Emma, are you okay?" Jason asked with honest concern, I could see his face was flushed with desire.

"Yeah, sorry, I thought I saw someone watching…" I trailed off with a face cornered with guilt, I started fidgeting with the carvings on the balcony.

"Oh, yeah sorry we were getting a bit carried away." Jason nodded, looking sympathetic.

"No, it's okay, I don't see anyone now." I started leaning forward. I was filled with desire but the guilt made me waver. *I just need more time to think this through.* Out of the corner of my eye I noticed a marble sculpture of upper torso and head of a man with a bowler's hat. It was resting on top of a mahogany wood pedestal with intricate letter carvings that read, '*The Man in The Green Hat*'.

"Look, Jason! This is the guy Andy was talking about! The badass booze dealer!"

Jason gave a laugh with delight as I walked straight over to the statue and started tinkering with it. He wanted to take pictures of me kissing the statue on the cheek. I agreed but on the condition that we would then both take pictures together with '*the man in the green hat*', giving our best '*we've been out partying all night*' look.

I then took a picture of Jason pretending to choke the statue. As he tried to lift its chin, he accidentally tilted its head back.

We were both standing back in shock as it looked like he had broken it.

But to our surprise, it turned out, it was a hidden switch which opened a trap door behind us, just like Bruce Wayne's access to the Batcave inside the Wayne Manor.

Jason and I jolted in excitement. We stepped in closer and peered into the room that was delicately opening before our eyes. It was dimly lit, but in a romantic way, with shelves full of old books, a rose gold gilded sofa, antique brass lamps, mahogany side tables, Persian carpets and a gold bar cart filled with whisky bottles and crystal glasses. The walls had luxurious wood paneling.

The room was private and intimate yet we can still hear the music playing from the outside as though we were having a secret affair in the midst of a very busy party. Jason led me to the sofa and sat down.

I wheeled around to face him. He bestowed a charming smile on me and unbuttoned his suit jacket.

This is quiet, and away from everybody enough. This is it... My New Year's Eve super fling! At this moment, this is just what I need. I am drowning in a sea of desire. *I want this. I need this. I just want us to satisfy each other. His lips... his breath... his touch will bring me back to life... It's just sex, we're both adults.*

Jason slowly reached inside his suit jacket's pocket and revealed what looked like a small custom painting - about the size of a postcard. He handed it to me. I felt hot under his gaze. I swallowed hard and tried to get hold of myself.

"I wanted to give this to you earlier..." Jason gave me a deep, earnest look.

It was a beautiful watercolor hand-painted card of a girl sitting on a chair by the balcony of a Haussmannian building. She had a blonde hair tied up in a pony, wearing a black turtleneck and was holding a ukulele. She was facing the majestic view of the *Eiffel Tower* overlooking the beautiful city around Paris.

There was some writing on the back which said:

'I hope you'll be here one day — writing compelling stories the world didn't know it needed.'

I was speechless. It was the most beautiful gift I'd ever received. He had put a lot of thought and effort into it, as though he knew me, knew my fantasy of becoming a writer. What I had always wanted to do. It was like he was encouraging me to be my best self – *my ideal self.*

"Thank you, Jason," I said after a few moments. "This is wonderful! I didn't know you could paint and draw."

"You're welcome." He seemed pleased that I loved his gift.

Jason slowly leaned forward inch by inch, and I felt a surge of anticipation as I closed my eyes with sudden passion. He ran his fingers through my hair. My heart was melting with every stroke of his hand.

He planted a warm kiss on my lips. I opened my mouth wanting more, my whole body tingled, begging for him to conquer every inch of me. I felt him caressing the side of my neck with soft and tender sucking that sent stimulating sensations down my spine. His soft lips and titillating breath ignited my carnal urges.

"I want you..." I whispered in his ear like a desperate plea for water after enduring a long, isolated misery in the Sahara desert. "Tell me what you want me to do to you, Jason..." I murmured as my hands ran over his chest and his broad shoulders.

"I don't know if that's appropriate for me to say..." He whispered, teasing me even more.

I opened my eyes and felt weak under his penetrating gaze. He stroked my face. I was intoxicated by his musk scent as adrenaline surged inside me.

With an animal instinct, I gathered up all my strength and pushed him back so I could climb on top of his lap. I stared into his deep ocean eyes and gave him a sly, mischievous smile.

For a moment, I felt like I was sitting at the peak of a roller coaster track, looking down to the thrilling ride that's about to start. I was scared yet thrilled with a pounding heartbeat and a stomach filled with butterflies. I knew the breathtaking freefall would be at an unstoppable, accelerated rate.

I leaned closer to Jason as I brushed my fingers on his cheeks. Our lips met and it was a visceral sensation of euphoria. I felt his desire grow underneath me as we kissed and ran our hands over each other. I slowly held the back of his head and tug his hair gently to break off our riveting rendezvous.

I pulled his suit jacket's lapel so that his body would partially cover mine, as we laid down side by side.

He softly kissed my neck down to my shoulders... His hand crawled down to the side of my thigh and started tracing up, higher and higher as I let out a soft moan of pleasure and anticipation. He slowly lifted the hem of my dress revealing a little bit more of my skin.

"I know everything's moving so fast... Emma, but truthfully I haven't stopped thinking about you... since the day we met." Jason whispered lightly in my ear.

"Really?" I breathed softly.

Our fingers toyed. His eyes were surging with passion.

"Emma, I think I'm falling for you... I want to be with you... if you feel the same... I don't want this to be about one night, I want to keep seeing you." He looked at me deeply, waiting for my response. After a few seconds, he swallowed hard.

For a dizzying few seconds, my face jolted in shock. My mind was whirling back in confusion.

Am I ready to move on to another relationship? I just broke up with Mark a couple of months ago... And I still think about him, hoping that we'll get back together when his temporary job is over.

I know that Mark and I didn't promise to wait for each other and there's a chance Mark had already fallen in love with someone else... But why does the thought of him still make my heart skip a beat? Is this just my own guilty conscience speaking?

Jason is falling for me. Can I say the same too? I haven't thought about it until now... tonight was just supposed to be a fling, but he wants to be with me. I kept running through all these different scenarios in my mind, about how I felt, and what I could maybe one day feel.

My heart dove into my stomach. There was a gleam in Jason's eyes and I felt myself getting lost in his look.

"Just kiss me, Jason... I want to spend *this* night with you..." I gazed over his face and searched his eyes.

"Look, I want nothing more than to make love to you right here, right now; but I know if I do that without knowing this, without asking... I want to know it this means more to you than just sex. Do you see yourself with me... for more than just one night? Do you see us being together?" Jason uttered softly.

I felt his chest heave with deep breathing as he waited for my response.

"Maybe, I mean perhaps eventually. I just... I can't say I'm sure right now." I said as my stomach lurched.

"Why is that... Don't you feel the same?" Jason looked back at me.

"I know I really like you, we always seem to have a great time together, but I... I don't think I'm ready for a serious relationship right now. I just broke up with my ex a couple of months ago." My mind whirled with confusion.

"I see. That would make it hard. The question is though, do you still love him?" Jason looked straight into my eyes, his cheeks were bright pink.

There was a bewildering silence between us as I took a deep breath to calm my nerves. Finally, I pressed my lips together and nodded lightly, afraid to look him in the eye.

"Do you really mean that? Tell me the truth Emma, I want to *hear* it from you. Do you still love him?" He paused and met my eyes as though giving me another chance.

"The truth is..." I trailed off, sighing deeply. "The truth is... yes, I still love him," As the words came out of my mouth, I saw the devastation on his face. "I'm so sorry, Jason. It's wrong for me to take things as far as they have, with someone I care about but can't return their sentiments..."

I felt like my whole facade I had carefully built up was crumbling away.

He drew a deep breath, looking down as though running over in his mind what he will say next. I longed to comfort him, to tell him that everything would be okay. But I sat there frozen.

"I see..." He said trying to sound calm. He forced a weak smile and slowly moved his body away from mine until he was sitting erect in the sofa looking at a blank space.

My face was covered with guilt. I said, "Honestly, I really like you... can we—"

"Emma... Maybe when you're ready, not hung up on some other guy." He said looking down at the floor. "Regardless, I had a lovely night with you. Definitely one of the many nights that I will never forget..."

Jason gazed at me wistfully.

"Jason, tonight was one of the best moments of my life... and it's mostly because of you." I murmured in my most jovial voice. I genuinely meant it as I felt my eyes prickling.

Jason stroked my cheek and tipped my chin up as he stared at my face for as long as he could muster.

"I have to go now, Emma." He said with a slight wobble in his voice.

Jason stood up to his feet, took a deep breath, and put his hands in his pockets. Before I realized it, he was walking to the door in silence.

"Wait!... Jason, please... come back..." I felt my eyes welling up with tears.

He stopped, but didn't look back.

"Maybe—" His voice shook a bit. "Maybe someday." He swiftly brushed his hand on his cheek.

He then left the room, shutting the door behind him.

I sat there with tears streaming down my cheeks. My throat was tight. Sitting on the cushiony sofa for a while, with the unbearable silence of the room as my only company. I felt a stabbing in my heart as I clasped my head in bewilderment.

Did I do the right thing by telling him the unvarnished truth? Why am I crying right now if I'm still in love with Mark? My mind added like a silent truthful arrow.

For a moment, I realized what Jason meant to me. He was like an angel watching over me ever since we first met. From giving me spare change for my chocolate cravings... to fixing my rickety old laptop, giving me a notebook to encourage my writing, saving me from cracking my head by the pool, inspiring me to conquer my fear of the unknown, patiently waiting until I finally jump into the pool, saving me from a creepy dude in school, writing me a lovely, sweet poem... All of this poured over me as I sat there wondering about what I had done.

He made my New Year's Eve special, he kissed me under the fireworks and put up with my silly thoughts of lucky superstitions, he danced with me with gentleness, kissed me passionately, he made a postcard painting of my dreams and aspirations. My mind went back and forth over the whole evening.

Why did I let him go?

I took the painting he gave me, got up to my feet, and ran after him. I went down the grand staircase and for the first time I felt resentment at how unnecessarily huge it was. I should have taken the gold birdcage elevator.

Finally, I spotted Andy! As I hurriedly sprinted my way toward him, I slipped and stumbled forward on the floor. I felt a searing pain in my ankle as I stood back up, I wasn't sure if it was twisted but I was too afraid to look.

I continued limping my way as fast as I could to Andy as I dragged my injured leg partially hunched over.

"Andy! Have you seen Jason? I need to find him!" I said in a choked voice as my eyes squinted from the bright light of the stage close by.

Andy's mouth dropped open in horror as he stared at me.

"My God! Emma, what happened? You look like the Hunchback of Notre Dame!"

"What? What do you mean?" I took a once-over of myself and realized that I indeed must have looked like Quasimodo.

"I fell down! It doesn't matter — Andy, have you seen Jason?" I blurted out in desperation.

"Oh honey, he already left. He said he had a flight to catch, or something along those lines, why? What happened?" Andy's brows wrinkled in worry as he surveyed my face.

"A flight? What?" I slumped down onto my knees, acutely aware of the throbbing pain in my ankle. "He told me that he was falling for me."

"Oh... I take it things didn't go well from there then?" Andy said as he knelt beside me.

"No, I was confused... I just... don't know how I feel exactly, everything felt so rushed," A cold feeling started to creep over me. I swallowed hard and looked up to Andy and confessed. "I told him I was still in love with my ex... Still in love with Mark" I whispered the last part as I closed my eyes.

I could feel a tight knot in my stomach, I just wanted this nightmare to be over.

Andy gave a comforting pat on my shoulder. "Honey, you did the right thing telling him the truth."

"But he's perfect Andy! He has always been there for me and now... Now I've lost him," I felt a pang of guilt well up inside me as I uttered those words. The stark reality of them hit me like a ton of bricks. Feeling powerless, I sat there letting the tears pour down my face. Andy looked stricken and dumbfounded.

"Andy... Can I have a hug?" I whispered softly.

"Oh, right! Of course! Here you go, love..." Andy wrapped his arms around me like a cuddly teddy bear. I sat there sobbing gently, burying my head into his shoulders.

"You smell nice, what is that?" I sniffled as I held on to him.

"Ha, my dear, it's my own combo — a light papaya extract conditioner paired with a lovely alcohol-free cologne against the cheek and neck. The cologne is a trade secret I'm afraid and I shall have to take it to the grave!" Andy chuckled.

"Well, whatever it is, it's working," I said, smiling through teary eyes.

"Emma Bray, what shall we do with you? Now I see that look in your eye, you wounded gazelle! But we're simply friends, okay? I know I'm hot, rich, and perfect... But I would never forgive myself!" Andy sniggered as I let out a small laugh.

"Thanks Andy, I just wish my heart didn't hurt so much," sighing as I held back on to him. "That and my friggin' ankle is killing me!"

"I can help my dear," He took a deep breath and yelled like a seasoned drama queen, "Somebody help my friend! She has a sprained foot and a broken heart! Bring ice! Both the cream and water varieties!"

And just like that, a small crowd of total strangers gathered around to comfort me.

"Thanks again Andy," I said with a sad smile. At least the ice cream was delicious.

Chapter Fourteen

Andy's Dilemma

I t was Valentine's day and I found myself yet again without a date, nor did I receive a call from any ex or potential lovers. I felt leaden all day. To distract myself I started actively looking for a job online so that I could start paying off the student loan debt I had acquired. With convocation pending in Spring, I would soon have to start chipping away at it.

After the disaster at the New Year's Eve party, I had tried to call Jason, but all of my phone calls to him were diverted to his voicemail. He would occasionally text me back in short, terse responses which all felt a little bit cold. So, I had given up trying to reconnect with him. He clearly didn't want to hear from me anymore, and I respected that. Why would he anyway, I practically broke his heart.

I still remembered our moments together whenever I drank club soda, or listened to my Etta James record, or whenever I would eat grapes or French bread. Every time I wrote new stories in the notebook he gave me, I'd read his acrostic poem he wrote for me. I even missed his scent.

To be fair, I also missed Mark. It was probably for the best that I wasn't with either of them at the moment since I couldn't really make up my mind. I just felt so confused, like a clueless dummy who would latch on to anyone who gave me love and attention. *Am I just a love whore?* I thought bitterly to myself. *Maybe I need to learn how to be alone.*

I was jolted out of my depressing reverie by the ringing on my apartment buzzer. I got up to check who it was as I was not expecting anyone to visit me. I was a little shocked when I found out it was a courier delivery for me.

The courier guy looked weirded out as he handed my package after I had signed for it. I shook my head wondering what his problem was until I caught a glimpse of myself in the mirror. There I stood in a light pink unicorn onesie with grey plush bunny slippers. Clearly, I had let myself go a little bit. *Good Lord, I hope I don't run into Andy or Laura, I will never hear the end of it!* I chuckled at the thought of them seeing me. As for the courier, well, it didn't matter what he thought about me. I was just too excited at having received something on Valentines Day!

I glanced down to see who had sent it and I was stunned. The package came from Mark! I quickly sat down on my couch and opened it, tearing up the box.

It was a record, a '*Dinah Washington*' vintage vinyl record that I had been searching for the longest time! *He remembered.* I thought warmly to myself.

There was also a card from Mark that was included, it read:

'Congratulations on graduating, Emma! I'm so proud of you! Happy Hearts Day! Hope to see you soon!'

-Mark'

From staring off in misery only moments ago, I was now smiling ear to ear, my heart was beating fast in my chest.

'Hope to see you soon!?' Does this mean Mark is coming back? It's only been four months since he left. I wonder if he wants to get back together. Maybe he realized how much he loves me, that he

misses me so much! Then we can start a life together... Maybe get married soon? Have kids... Buy a house, a minivan and a cottage by the lake! I wonder when he'll be back... Maybe I should call him! Maybe he'll call me... My mind raced as thoughts of Mark and I moving forward filled me with joy and anticipation. I sat there, holding on to the card, thinking of our future when out of the blue, my phone rang. Picking up my cell, I looked and saw that it was Andy.

"Andy!" I yelled before he could even say hello. "You wouldn't believe—".

"Emma!" Andy interrupted me. "You've got to help me! My life is ruined!" Andy's voice was a penetrating shriek.

"What?! What do you mean? What's going on? Where are you?" I felt a genuine surge of panic.

"They found out! Kicked me out... My credit cards have been cut... I'm at some seedy motel on the edge of town, Emma! The horror!" Andy sobbed into a total meltdown.

"Sorry, who's they?" I asked trying to figure out what Andy was talking about.

"My parents, Emma, they found out everything," He sobbed again into the phone.

"Damn Andy, I'm so sorry! Where are you? I can pick you up right away!" My voice was shrill. I grabbed my bag and keys in five seconds flat, waiting for Andy to let me know where he was in the city. It didn't matter that I didn't have a car, I was going to take the bus wearing a pink unicorn onesie with plush bunny slippers.

"Emma, I'm... I'm in L.A. Please help me! All my friends are ignoring my calls... I feel like they've abandoned me Emma, I don't have any money, and I can't seem to get a hold of anyone, and I just don't know what to do," Andy's voice pierced my heart.

"Well I won't abandon you Andy, not while I'm still alive. I can transfer you some money so you can fly back here or even just buy the tickets for you," I said reassuringly.

"No, I can't... I can't leave LA. Not yet, I have to take care of something. I'm sorry Emma, I just. I don't want to bother you, I just needed to talk. I wish you were here, really." Andy whispered softly, as though to himself.

"Andy, stay where you are... I'm on my way!" I quickly hung up before he could respond and opened my laptop. I booked the earliest flight to Los Angeles and shoved a few clothes in my backpack. This time, I changed into a decent comfortable travel outfit. Although a onesie would have been perfect for the cold, red-eye flight.

I arrived at the LAX airport and took a rental car to get to Andy's motel. Never in a million years would I have thought Andy would be staying in a single-story building with ten rooms renting by the hour that had a sign that was still rocking a *with color TV* sign as a selling point. There was a chop shop and a strip club within fifty feet of the motel.

When I pulled up right in front of Andy's room in the motel parking lot, he came out with a tense smile and frightened eyes. I walked towards him, trying my best to make him feel relieved whilst looking around in disbelief.

"Ohh, thank God! Emma! You came! And you have a car! Let's get out of here!" Andy looked pleadingly as he threw his arms around me.

"Hey Andy, are you okay? Have you eaten? You don't look well," I frowned as I felt the distress in his voice.

"Ohhh, is it that bad, Emma? I haven't been able to sleep, my next door neighbor kept moaning and screaming all night, every night! I don't know if it's sexual or what! And the bed is rock-hard, I may as well lie down on the carpet... the air conditioner doesn't work, I doubt the sheets have ever been washed, the toilet was clogged... and worst of all - Worst. Of.

All... there's no Wi-Fi! I mean, can you believe that? What kind of place doesn't even have Wi-Fi?!" His voice was squeaky with nerves.

Andy didn't have anything of his stuff with him except his wallet and the clothes on his back. He wasn't kidding when he said he had nothing. My friend needed me badly and I could tell that he felt a bit relieved that I came for him. We went out to get some burgers and fries at a drive-through. Parked outside in a well-lit parking lot, Andy looked like he had been starving for days as he gobbled it all up in two minutes flat.

"We can get more if you want...." I said in a faint voice.

Andy tilted his face away as his eyes welled up.

"It's okay, Andy... I'm here... we'll sort this out... don't worry anymore, okay?" I said, holding his hand.

"I just... I didn't know what to do, Emma... they shunned me..." Andy's voice was barely above a whisper. "My own parents never want to see me again... all because... I'm gay..." His head dropped into his hands.

"Tell me everything..." I said, holding his hand firmly.

"I came here to L.A. to see my parents at our house in Beverly Hills for my *annual allowance review* — it's like, uh, a performance review at a regular job." Andy drew a breath trying to recall his traumatic experience.

"That sounds... awful, I'm sorry, go on." I said tactfully.

"Tell me about it. Anyway, I was meeting with my mom, dad and an accountant to review my expenses for the past year. They were all impressed by how much I kept my expenses in line, you know... I didn't buy more than one car and took only one trip to the South of France. They all agreed to give me a fifteen percent raise on my allowance for this year." Andy sounded slightly delighted.

I sank into my seat quietly as I moved my eyes incredulously at him.

He has no idea what life is like outside his bubble.

"So, I celebrated of course by going to my favorite gay bar in West Hollywood. I mean, gay bars are supposed to be our safe haven, how was I supposed to know that my salty *ex*-girlfriend will be there in a bachelorette party?" Andy said in a contemptuous tone.

"Okay, wait, back up... ex-girlfriend? *Please explain.*" I looked meaningfully at him.

"We've known each other for a long time, since tenth grade, really. This girl had a huge crush on me for years, all through high school. Then one day, on my first year at the university, she caught me with another guy! She said she would tell everyone, and I knew my parents would find out, so I lied and told her that it was just a phase and that it was her I really liked. She believed me, and so we "dated". I even bought her fancy gifts and took her to nice places — all that jazz!" Andy's voice was indignant.

"Wow, you dated a girl? Did you kiss and... have sex?" I gaped at him like a moron.

"What? Gawd no, ew! Yes, we kissed but never had sex!" He said shooting me a look.

"Okay! Alright! Just hard to imagine." I laughed a bit.

"Well, try not to! As I was saying, after a few weeks, I couldn't live the lie anymore. I gently broke it off with her and she was obviously devastated. I felt awful, but at the same time I didn't know what to do. So, I made my peace with her and that was that, or so I thought."

"I was out and about last week, having a great time smooching with a hot, handsome Cuban go-go dancer at a dark corner of the bar when I noticed her standing right there. She gawked at us making out and took a video! She was drunk and was yelling at me, saying I had broken her heart."

"Maybe she had really fallen for you." I said trying not to gabble.

"She sent the video to everyone we know! It got into my parents' hands! They summoned me and asked me why I'm gay!

How could anyone answer that? I should have asked them why they're straight!" Andy sobbed uncontrollably.

He looked outside the window reminiscing about the most painful confrontation of his life.

"Then they asked me over and over... '*Are you sure you're gay?*'" Andy swiftly brushed off the tears falling down his cheeks. "And when I said I knew I was gay since I was twelve... Then they shouted at me: '*You're gonna die of AIDS!*'," His voice was rising and becoming restless. "They're so homophobic and closed-minded!" His voice shrieked of anguish and heartache.

I threw my arms around Andy without a flicker and we were silent for a moment.

"They told me not to come back unless I'm not gay anymore! As if who I am is some disease I must cure! Why can't they understand... Why can't they just accept me?" He started to cry in my shoulders as I held him tight.

CHAPTER FIFTEEN

Mark's Confession

Andy and I checked into a decent three-star hotel with two comfortable double beds. It was quiet with no screaming lovers next door, clean with fresh linens, and the cherry on top was the working WiFi. The location felt safe with nearby coffee shops, grocery stores, and restaurants. I collapsed on the bed the moment we stepped into the room, so exhausted from my flight and lack of sleep. Andy on the other hand, drowned his sorrows and fears with an hour-long bubble bath. I tried to stay awake for him but I couldn't, I just passed out before he even got out.

I woke up the next morning feeling well-rested from a good night's sleep, stretching my arms above my head and rubbing my eyes as I sat up. My gaze landed at Andy's face smiling in a weird yoga position on the floor.

"Good morning, sleepyhead! Had a good night's sleep?" He chuckled at me. I stared back at him as he slowly contorted his body with his arms squeezed under his thighs like a frog suspended mid-air.

'What the...' I silently mouthed, completely baffled.

"Jealous?" Said Andy coyly. "Don't be — not everyone can do the *Bhujapidasana* pose..." Andy looked triumphant as he held his position.

"Actually, I am a little bit." I nodded as I stared. "We should go to the free continental breakfast soon before we miss it!" I glanced warningly at him.

"What? Why? They have room service," Andy said calmly.

"No, Andy! We can't afford room service... we gotta get to the free breakfast buffet and fill up so we don't have to buy lunch!" I sounded desperate as I started getting dressed to head out.

"Alright, well I am dying for some fluffy *brioches* and some delicious *pains au chocolat* anyway." Andy got up with eyes shining brightly.

"Yes, of course dear. I'm sure they'll have that." I couldn't help but giggle at the thought of him expecting delicate French pastries in the hotel we're staying in.

As we descended down the stairs into the lobby where the free breakfast buffet was provided, I saw a brief flinch in Andy's face as we perused the buffet selection. An eclectic mix of scrambled eggs, sausage, white bread, waffles, hash browns, bananas, apples, orange juice, herbal tea and coffee — not quite French cuisine. To my surprise, he didn't complain nor made any comment about the food. I grabbed a plate and piled up all the food I could, as if I had some starving family of four holding a table for me, while Andy picked up a modest amount. *Sucker.* I thought as we sat down together. *Wait until he's hungry later and I'm still full off the twelve pieces of bacon... maybe I took too much.*

"Hmmmm... this is so good!" I sounded breezy as my eyes snapped open at the waffles with maple syrup. Andy took a bite of sausage and made a so-so gesture with his hand. As I was staring blankly at the window, an idea flashed into my mind.

"Andy! I'm in L.A.!" I swiveled around dramatically like a lunatic.

"Yes, yes you are. What have you been smoking? And may I have some too?" Andy surveyed me with fascination.

"Andy, Mark's in L.A.! We can meet and talk. He just mailed me a graduation gift! And wrote — *'see you soon'* on the card! Well, I'm here! I can certainly see him now!" I was feeling bubbly with exhilaration thinking of enticing possibilities between Mark and myself.

"Oh, how wonderful! If you two, do get back together it'll be of some comfort to know it was because of my tragedy," Andy's voice was teasing as he clasped his hands together.

"You're the best Andy, I'm going to text him, or maybe I should *call* him!" I said, clearly getting carried away.

"Uhm, call him? My gawd woman, have we stepped back in time? Just *text* him!" Andy looked squeamish.

"Whatever Andy, calling's more personal but I'll just *text* him," I rolled my eyes at him as I started texting Mark.

I let him know that I was in Los Angeles to help Andy. He quickly responded back and agreed to meet me at a coffee shop near our hotel. I instantly became excited and yet extremely nervous. I was almost hyperventilating in panic thinking of what could happen in just a few hours.

"Andy, is it cool if I just meet Mark later for coffee?" I asked, with the most pleading look I could muster.

"And you'll leave me in my time of distress for some *guy*!" Andy turned his head in mocking hurt.

"Andy, it's not some guy! Besides, there's lots to do around here!" I said half laughing at his display.

"Oh of course hun! I'll be fine, enjoy your rendezvous! I shall see about what type of spa treatments this hotel has." He paused reading the hotel brochure. "Hmm, I see, well I suppose I'll just sit in the tub with some cucumbers on my face. Have fun and say hi to Mark for me!" Andy got up and walked back towards the room. My heart was pounding at the thought of meeting Mark again, I couldn't wait!

As I walked towards the coffee shop, I couldn't believe it. I was going to see Mark again.

My heart was thumping as I stepped into the café, trying to gather my wits. It didn't take long to find Mark at a corner table in the room. His gaze was fixed on mine as I strode to him. Within moments, we were facing each other with sunshine from the window illuminating his face.

"Hi, Mark..." I heard myself say. I met his eyes and felt shivers down my spine.

"Hello, Emma..." His face was suffused with color as he gave me a bewitching smile.

I felt myself slip into a trance, as hope for some happiness with him again elated me. In an instant, our past romance rehashed before my eyes. The way his fingers brushed my hair. How we kissed under the big bright moon in the dark. How we made love passionately. How he used to whisper in my ear, pull me toward him and captivate me with his penetrating eyes.

I couldn't help but notice that Mark looked different. He was wearing a sharp navy blue suit with a matching silk full Windsor tie. His shoes were brown polished Oxford brogues, and his hair was finely combed through in a slicked-back style.

Mark sat there and studied my face for a few moments. Leaning in closer, he asked me what I would like to drink. I asked for a *café latte* and Mark had an *Americano.* We sat back down in the small, wooden chairs with round tables.

"Thank you for the graduation gift." I said as my nerves finally returned.

"You're welcome, it reminded me of you when I saw it. I had to get it for you," Mark paused thoughtfully as he ran his fingers along the side of his cup.

Mark looked dressy and sharp for an afternoon coffee date. Deep down inside I missed the way he used to dress - like a laid-back, carefree guy. I was taken aback by how business-like he was dressed up but truthfully, I was also mesmerized by how handsome he looked as though he was a man of power and wealth.

"Nice suit, Mark. Were you in a meeting with some film execs?" I smiled and took a sip of my latte.

"Huh, no," Mark gave a soft laugh "Change of plans happened, I've been working at my uncle's brokerage firm. I ditched the film-editing job. It just didn't work out, and to be honest I feel like I'm done with film." He said with a distancing smile as his eyes flashed.

"Oh, sorry to hear that, I know how much it meant to you, but congrats on the new gig! So, how long have you been at your new job?" I was astounded but I tried to sound light. He was no longer pursuing his passion and he didn't even mention it to me after all this time. There was a strong silence between us, and I shot him a reproachful look.

"Uhm, I just started really..." Mark's face changed as he trailed off, looking dazed.

"But why, Mark? I thought you said filmmaking was your passion. It's what you've always wanted to do, and it's the reason why you came to L.A... the reason... the reason why we had to break up," My words flew out as I stared at him, stricken.

"Emma, things have changed."

I saw his worried eyes scanning my face. He massaged his temples briefly, as if searching for something to say.

"I see, and were you ever going to tell me if I hadn't come here?" I said annoyed at him.

"Yes... I mean, I just, I didn't know how..." Mark looked away. His face crumpled in distress. I felt a twinge of sadness as I took a few deep breaths, trying to calm my nerves.

"Mark, I know we've broken up, and I don't have any right to pry into your life or make you tell me whatever it is that caused you to change your mind, but I just thought you'd at least let me know, as your friend." I said after a moment's consideration.

"Emma, I've made a..." Mark's voice started to sound hoarse. "I don't know how..." He continued in a strangled voice looking aghast.

"What is it, Mark? You can tell me." I said as I took a miserable slug of my coffee, fearing his answer.

"I met someone here, another girl, and we spent a few nights together. Emma, this girl, she's... she's pregnant with my child." he murmured as he buried his face with his hands.

"But... when? Why didn't you tell..." I clapped a hand over my mouth.

Mark's face was cornered with guilt.

"My colleagues and I went to a bar, and I met a girl that night. We spent some time together, hooking up and what not... Then two months later, she called me and told me she's pregnant and that I'm the dad and that she was keeping it. She said I could be as involved as I liked and that I didn't owe her anything, but I wasn't going to abandon her. It was just all so sudden, I didn't know what to do, I had to find a job that would support my child. I had to quit the film-editing gig and grow up." Tears flooded his face. He shook his head in exasperation.

In shock, I stared blankly at him. There was a long excruciating silence as I tried to process his confession. I closed my eyes and just like that, all my fantasies melted away. My face was boiling hot, I was an emotional wreck. The possibility of him becoming a father never had even crossed my mind. I felt tears brimming in my eyes. I was not able to contain the pain that abruptly struck my heart. Blood was pulsating around my head. I felt like slapping him.

But then I also felt a stab of sympathy for him, the girl and his unborn child. Although I was still in love with him, I knew that it would never be the same between us. I knew we were no longer together, but I still hoped that there was a chance for us to be together again. What made me feel even worse was that I drove Jason away because I was still in love with someone who had already moved on and then got another woman pregnant.

I swallowed hard and took a deep sigh. I just wanted to leave right then and there.

"I see... well, it was nice to see you again, Mark. I hope everything goes well." I forced a smile then got up out of my chair. "I have to go, Andy's waiting for me in the hotel."

"Emma, can you stay for a bit longer?" Mark reached for my hand and squeezed it tight.

"No, I'm sorry, I have to go." I slowly pried my hand out of his.

"Emma, I love you... You're the one I want to be with... I just need to figure out how to make this work. I got a high-paying job to support my child. The mother and I don't want to be together. We're just trying to sort this out." He said, looking remorseful with a wobbly voice.

"I... I just wish you hadn't kept this from me for months. I think I just need to be by myself for a while."

To my surprise, I genuinely meant what I said. I knew that his child needed him more than I did. I kept my chin up and started walking out the door without looking back.

My shoulders were hunched in disappointment and my legs were trembling as I emerged out of the café, standing in the middle of the pavement. I kept walking until I found a nearby park bench where I sat, crying in silence. I realized that I needed to reorder my priorities in life.

When I came back to the hotel, our room was full of clothes everywhere, with three full-sized suitcases on the floor.

"Oh My God, Emma, are you okay? What happened to you? Andy asked looking worried.

"I'll tell you everything later." I replied, feeling a bit shame-faced. "Andy, whose clothes are these?" I asked in puzzlement examining the expensive-looking cardigans and pants with ultra-soft fabrics.

"Well, our butler – Ed, came by and dropped off some of my clothes, accessories, toiletries and skincare products I had left in my parents' house." Andy's eyes crinkled in a smile.

"But Andy, we can't bring all of these... we'll be paying lots for check-in baggage!" I eyed him with apprehension.

"But Ed gave me some cash, he had been worried about me. And if I'm being honest, he's been more of a father figure than my actual dad, he practically raised me since both of my parents were always traveling. He knows that I'm gay for the longest time... Ed treats me like his son. He said he'll send me more money next month, without my parents knowledge of course."

"Andy, you can't keep taking money from Ed. Plus you're going to need some cash for school, food and other stuff since your parents, you know, cut you off..." I eyed him suspiciously.

He stared at me in bewilderment for a few seconds, then drew himself up, and put his best face forward with a smile.

"Oh, and Emma, one more thing, I can't step foot in my condo... so, I'm going to have to live with you, Ems! Sounds good? I mean, you really are the lucky one," Andy uttered with a grimace on his face.

I stared at him for a few silent seconds, utterly dumbfounded.

"You're going to be okay living in a tiny studio apartment with me?" I stared at him incredulously.

"Well, I'd rather be in a penthouse at the *Chateau Marmont* but sadly, I can't really afford it at this moment..." Andy gazed back at me with a jocular smile.

Andy and I got to the airport the next day to head back home. To be fair to him, he has never traveled in economy class before. Our seats were all the way in the back of the plane.

"Emma, I can't move my legs... we should have at least booked *Business Class*." Andy said in a piercing voice.

I gave Andy a look of horror, which made him silent for a while, surprisingly.

Out of the blue, he pressed the button to call the attention of a flight attendant.

"Champagne please... and will you be serving caviar with it?" Andy craned his neck, looking confident ordering what he usually would feast on during a flight.

People in front of us looked back and peered at Andy. So did the man right next to me.

"Andy, those are not complimentary in *coach*. Just get a free glass of ginger ale and some saltine crackers." I said in reproach.

I spent most of the flight running over Mark's situation in my mind. I could barely keep it together, but thankfully Andy never pried once. After a long, agonizing flight, and what seemed like an even longer cab ride, we finally arrived at my apartment.

Exhausted, Andy sat on the sofa and started looking around.

"Where's your bed, Emma? I'm dead tired. I wouldn't mind heading to bed if that's alright with you?" He closed his eyes as he let out a big yawn.

"My bed? You're sitting on it!" I met his gaze as I raised my eyebrows.

Andy turned pale with shock and gasped with his hand on his mouth.

"You're kidding! Your sofa is also your bed?!" He looked dumbfounded as I stood him up and began removing the cushions to reveal the bottom platform of the sofa that would pull out into a bed.

"Wow, I would have never thought there'd be a whole bed tucked under here. But better than the pavement... so alright, good night, Ems!" Andy claimed his spot and tucked a pillow under his head.

"Oh, and there's only supposed to be one tenant in this studio, so try to hide from the building caretaker or at least act like you were just visiting when you see him, okay?" I added as an afterthought just to be safe.

"Okay, alright. I'll tell him I'm just here to shag you on the weekends, with you being all lonely." Andy bantered with one eye open.

"Great, at least now he'll know why I look constantly disappointed. Oh, are you hungry? Did you want anything to eat?" I said, turning to face him.

"Oh, my dear, I would blow your mind. But never mind, for food, what do you have? And please don't tell me instant noodles!" He uttered half asleep.

"Uhm, instant noodles... but they're the fancy kind! The ones that come with a packet of sesame oil!" I said proudly without a flicker.

"Oh, I didn't know such divine food existed, a sesame oil packet, I'm okay though, just need some rest." Andy mumbled as he crossed both his arms over his chest like a vampire.

CHAPTER SIXTEEN

Baby's Breath Bouquet

Mom had invited me to spend the weekend at her house along with Jackson for Mother's Day. He was also bringing his girlfriend, Maureen, so I thought I'd bring Andy along with me as my plus one.

That Friday afternoon I went to the mall to get my mom some beautiful spring flowers at a flower shop. I had a bit of time before I had to be at my mom's house, so I leisurely perused the nicely arranged floral arrangements and bouquets. I leaned closer to inhale the mesmerizing scents from fresh-cut roses, tulips, lilacs, peonies, daisies and chrysanthemums, when out of the blue, I heard a familiar voice.

"Emma..." Said a soft, bashful voice from behind me.

I stiffened in apprehension. There was a flip in my stomach as my heart was thumping. I recognized the voice instantly. I slowly turned around to face him.

"Jason! what.. where... " I stumbled over my words as I pretended to cough, feeling embarrassed.

"Hey! Good to see you. Are you okay?" His face lit up with glee in an obvious effort to suppress a chuckle.

"Yeah, sorry! Just having a 'lil stroke." I bantered as I felt my face flush slightly.

His eyes locked on mine as I gazed at him intensely with my mouth slightly parted. "So, buying flowers for someone?" Jason's eyes glittered for a moment with an endearing smile.

"Oh, yeah, they're for my mom. You know, Mother's Day." I said frustrated with myself. *God, I wish I had done my hair better!* I thought, cursing myself for rushing earlier in the morning.

The last time I saw Jason was on New Year's Eve, and that didn't end well for both of us. I was a bit flummoxed at seeing him again so I just kept sniffing the flowers around.

Surprisingly, Jason was trailing behind me as though he was bemused of my uncanny behavior. Maybe he just wanted to make sure that I didn't break anything inside the flower shop.

I swiveled back around without caution and ended up bumping against him. It was a total accident, I swear! Regardless, I caught a whiff of his cologne, and I instantly lost my senses. I quickly concocted a plan in my head to be closer to him, so I exaggerated a jolt and pushed myself forward against his chest. He caught my arms to prevent me from "falling". Yes, it wasn't one of my proudest moments, but hey, it worked!

"Oh, I'm sorry." I said in a barely concealed murmur.

"That's alright. Are you hurt?" He chimed in urgently.

"No, I'm fine! Thanks." I felt powerless as he surveyed me from head-to-toe.

I jerked my chin up and swallowed hard, trying to control my own faculties. I stood back up and looked around the shop, when suddenly my eyes laid upon a bouquet filled with pink peonies wrapped in light pink tissue papers. It was enchanting, like '*The Secret Garden*' bundled up together for anyone's taking. It was also the last bouquet of pink peonies available for sale that day.

I opened my bag to take my wallet out, but it wasn't there. I was about to panic when I realized that I had left it on top of the fridge at home. Further cursing my luck, I searched for my jean pockets and luckily, I found a twenty-dollar bill. *Twenty dollars should be enough for a nice bouquet of flowers.*

I smiled and nodded at Jason knowingly as though saying. '*I got this*'.

I surveyed the wrapper and searched for the price tag. My heart sank as I looked down, it was *fifty dollars.*

Fifty dollars for some peonies and roses! Damn, they are absolutely beautiful. I bet my mom would love those. I should have known that they'd be pricey since it's Mother's Day. I stood there with the flowers in hand, running over my options.

I looked up and saw Jason smile at me. I rummaged through other bouquets and floral arrangements looking for anything that was less than twenty dollars including tax. I then discovered that I could only walk away with a bundle of Baby's-breath. *Dammit!*

My heart sank slightly, this was to be my first Mother's Day with my mom and I really wanted to buy the most beautiful flowers for her, but that was that. So, I gathered my wits and decided that I'd go home as soon as possible.

I turned around and Jason was already holding that last bouquet of peonies walking towards the cashier. *Oh my god, oh my god, oh my god! Did he see me look over them? Does he know I don't have any cash on me and now he's going to buy them for me!* I felt giddy with excitement as I hurried to get closer to him.

"Who are you getting those flowers for?" I asked Jason with a knowing but hopeful tone. *This is it—*

"This girl that I'm... seeing."

"Oh... you have a girlfriend?" I interrupted softly as I stared at him, stricken. My little daydream of him saving me once more shattered before my eyes as he spoke.

He swiveled around with a pitying look on his face as I stood there staring in disbelief, feeling a lump in my throat. I couldn't cry, I couldn't breathe, I just couldn't. *He has a girlfriend now. And he's giving her the most beautiful pink peonies. That bouquet is supposed to be mine. He's supposed to be mine.* I thought bitterly.

On the brink of a meltdown and for no good reason, I uttered with a voice cracking with emotion, "Oh, sorry, I saw those first! I was gonna put it on hold —"

"We actually don't put flowers on hold, Miss. First come, first served. Sorry." Chimed in the shop attendant as she came to assist Jason.

"Uh, no it's okay, she can." Jason started.

"But, but I was going to leave a down payment! See! Here's twenty dollars... Then I'll be back in half an hour! I had just forgotten my wallet!" I yelled interrupting Jason, feeling slightly wrong-footed.

"Sorry, Miss. We don't take down payments either, and this customer is ready to pay and go." The shop attendant stared at me pityingly.

I felt a tiny spike of frustration. Then I caught sight of other customers standing around gaping at me as though I was some escaped mental patient.

"It's okay Em, I'll just get something else." Jason looked at me with that horrible pitying look again.

"No, I'm okay. Sorry, Uhm... I'll just get a bundle of *Baby's-breath* please." I gave my twenty-dollar bill, picked up my "flowers", and walked out of the store with hunched shoulders. I didn't dare look back at Jason out of extreme embarrassment.

I trudged through the exit door of the mall hollow and dispirited. I felt embarrassed, ashamed, and stupid. But worst of all, I felt remorse. And I knew it wasn't really about the flowers.

I walked into my apartment with the bundle of sad baby's breath under my arms, feeling defeated. Slumping down onto the couch, I hadn't even bothered to take my shoes off.

"Hey, Emma, I'm just about ready to... Oh my god, are you okay?" Andy came out from the bathroom, his hair filled with an assortment of products.

"Huh? Oh, yeah, sorry. Just a little out of it." I lied, I didn't exactly feel like talking about what had happened earlier.

"Well you look awful dear. Oh, are those the flowers?" Andy bent down and picked them up. "Um, Emma, aren't baby's breath supposed to go *with* the flowers?" Andy asked with his eyebrows raised.

"Yeah I know, I just forgot my stupid wallet at home and all I had was twenty bucks on me." I said slumping further into the couch. *Could this day get any worse?* I thought bitterly.

"Oh! Well we certainly can't be giving your mom *flower garnish* for Mother's Day." Andy said with a slight smile. "But no need to worry, I picked up some nice pink daisies earlier so we can just put them together!"

I nodded in agreement and rolled over onto my side. I didn't have the energy nor will to banter back with Andy. Truthfully, all I wanted to do was get into my comfiest pajamas and crawl into bed, staying there all day.

"Are you sure you're okay Emma, I mean we can just give her the baby's breath if you want? Is that some sort of inside joke or sentiment between the two of —"

"I saw Jason today at the Flower shop!" I blurted out loud, putting my hands over my face.

"Oh..." Andy said as he sat down beside me.

"He... he was picking up some flowers for somebody else — a girl he is seeing," I confessed as he put his arm around my shoulders and comforted me. "Goddammit Andy! I just wish... I wish I didn't look so pathetic. You should have seen the way he looked at me, but what can I do? I drove him away!" I muttered bitterly.

"Hey, it's okay, it's okay." Andy squeezed me. "I'm sorry Emma, I know this sucks. And I'm sorry I have no words of wisdom right now, but I'm here. You're like my best friend, and you've done a lot for me. I'll never leave your side, I'll always be in your corner, so we can reschedule with your mom if you'd like? Get some chocolate ice cream, and watch *Love Actually, Bridget Jones's Diary,* or whatever rom-com you want to get you through this. I'll be here." He smiled at me warmly.

I buried my face into his shoulders, he smelled so nice. I wanted so badly to just laze around the apartment with Andy all day but I had promised my mom I would be coming over and I didn't want to let her down.

"Thanks so much, Andy," I said wiping a tear away. "But I'd like to go, I told my mom I would. Maybe we could do that when we get back?" I said with a soft sigh.

"Sounds good to me hun," Andy smiled at me.

"And Andy?" I said, staring into his eyes.

"Yeah hun?" Andy looked back at me with concern.

"It's *Predator*... *Predator* is my go-to movie when I'm getting over a heartache."

"Seriously?" Andy laughed at me with a bemused look in his eyes.

"Shut up!" I laughed back, hitting him with a pillow, smiling for the first time in a while. "There's *something* about that monster really gets me, you know."

"Whatever weirdo, let's go!" Andy laughed, rolling his eyes as we sat up and left.

CHAPTER SEVENTEEN

Convocation

We arrived at mom's house and were greeted by an appetizing aroma of home-made cooking. Mom always had help around the house, but she recently learned how to cook for us under the direction of a good friend. The scrumptious dinner made my mouth water, and my stomach rumbled like a roaring lion.

My mom made chicken cordon bleu, Cajun shrimp pasta, roast beef, mashed potatoes and caprese salad. Bottles of wine were overflowing on the table with various cheese and freshly baked French baguettes. For dessert, we had crème brûlée and French macarons. I loved that mom had put in so much effort into making dinner for us. She told me that she'd even teach me how to cook if I'd come over more often to visit her.

After dinner, mom led me to the drawing room and pointed at the picture frames on the wall.

"I'd like you to see the new pictures I'd hung up." She said, her feet were springy as we strode to them.

It took me by surprise. There on the family gallery wall was a candid photo of me, mom and Jackson by the piano, singing our hearts out. Next to it was a solo frame of me smiling brightly — I couldn't even remember when and how that was taken but I was glad that I lucked out on a good angle. For the first time in a long while, I felt like I belonged to my family's home. I wasn't a stranger anymore. There was visible proof that I was part of their life.

"There'll be more pictures of us as time goes by." She said as though seized by inspiration.

"Mom, thank you. This means so much to me." I uttered, feeling tears rising in me.

"I'm glad you liked it." Mom's head jerked up, there was a trance look in her eyes as she gave me a warm hug.

"Well, let's take more pictures!" Andy chimed in and gave me an endearing smile. "Next time, I'll be on the gallery wall too!" His face lit up in good spirits while posing with plump pouty lips.

We took tons of new family pictures — me, mom, Jackson, his girlfriend Maureen and my plus one, Andy. Jackson brought out the good old Monopoly board game. I didn't stand a chance. I was first to have gone bankrupt and penniless, with not even a single property to mortgage. The game hit close to home and got too real - I wanted to flip the board as I burn the dice for always landing on bad luck. But of course, mom won. It was too easy for her as though taking candies from a bunch of helpless babies in soiled diapers. It got more entertaining when I caught Andy cheating red-handed and mom lawyered him up as though he was a hardened criminal.

Mom showed me her bedroom. It was very neat and minimalistic. The walls, ceiling and her bed covers were white as snow. All her French Provincial furniture — vanity, chaise lounge sofa, dresser and bed frame were also white with minimal gold trimmings. As opposed to the rest of the house, her curtains were sheer white and breezy. I liked the fact that she's not a hoarder of a million little porcelain trinkets or creepy dolls.

I loved my mom's room. Standing there right next to her made us feel closer together.

"I have something just for you." Mom's face glowed with cheerfulness.

Mom opened her vanity drawer and brought out a gold-plated jewelry box. She slowly pulled out the contents one by one and showed me her diamond necklaces, bracelets, and earrings.

"All of these are going to be yours one day." Mom gestured over to her precious jewelry collection. "Do you like them?" She gave me a little smile.

"They're beautiful, mom... But I'm not really into expensive jewelry." I said looking bewildered by her sparkling treasures. I was suddenly a little embarrassed that I was wearing a pair of fake diamond studs from *Claire's*. I was sure mom noticed that they were *faux* but she didn't say anything which made me more conscious about it.

"Jackson knows that I'll be passing these to you when I'm gone one day." Mom shot me a quick grin.

"Don't say that mom!" I raised my eyebrows tensely. "I don't want any jewelry, I just want to be with you!" I looked at her with concern.

"Yes, of course my child." Mom paused for a few seconds then added, "But nobody lives forever. I just want you to know that you'll be taken care of if one day, I suddenly flatlined." Mom shrugged casually.

"Precious jewelry will be the last thing on my mind in case that happens." I leaned forward and put my hand on her shoulder.

Mom took out a turquoise-colored box with satin white ribbon.

"I'm so proud of you for graduating, Emma! This is my little gift for you." Mom's eyes glittered as she handed me my graduation gift.

Mom wanted us to go to my commencement ceremony altogether as a family. I was not expecting any gift for marching on stage to receive a piece of paper. But I was truly happy that I received a present from mom for the very *first time in my entire life.*

I stared at the box and a look of confusion deepened inside me.

"Tiffany & Co. Mom, this is too much." I said bashfully.

"You're worth it, love. Open it!"

I slowly untied the satin ribbon around the box to see what's inside. It was an exquisite silver stainless steel watch. It was also personalized in the back with my engraved initials, '*E.B.*'

"I love it, mom! Thank you so much! I've never gotten anything like this before!" I said with a wobbled voice as I threw my arms around her.

"You're welcome, darling. I'm glad you liked it." She smiled at me lovingly and held me tight.

I was overflowing with joy.

I couldn't have asked for anything more than finally experiencing my mother's gentle love. Mom and I spent hours talking as she shared her most challenging moments in law school and newbie years as a full-fledged lawyer. I was enamored by her tenacity and wit. I wished I had her confidence. She told me stories from her childhood and how my grandparents raised her, which was exactly how they raised me too.

Time flew by and I ended up resting my head over my mom's lap in her bed as she softly smoothed back my hair. I curled up like a four-year old child partially falling asleep to bedtime stories. I never had any childhood experience with my mom but I felt like her sincere gestures made up for her shortcomings in the past. The clouds of happiness were over me and it was pouring so much love and joy as I basked in them.

Out of the blue, I whispered with my eyes closed. "I love you so much, mom." I heard mom replied with voice cracking with emotion. "I love you too, my child. I love you so much." I felt her hand go up and move in a sweeping motion across her face to wipe tears from her eyes.

I found myself in an ocean of black caps and togas sitting as a participant on one of the most important days of my life. My family and friends were all there to witness my convocation day. It was at this moment when it hit me. It's over, really over. I've dreaded the sleepless nights of studying, tiring days of going to class and stressing about grades after final exams.

Completing my degree took five years of my life. Five years of working part-time and going to University at the peak of my young adulthood.

I was still and silent experiencing a plethora of emotions on this *big day*. My mind was wandering to another dimension as the long inspirational speech was drowned by my own loud thoughts echoing inside my brain. I was relieved that I've finally reached the end of the finish line and I was happy to have achieved an important milestone. At the same time, I was feeling overwhelmed and anxious about what's going to happen next in my life.

I don't want my fear of failing to be greater than my desire to succeed in pursuing my dream. Because in order to achieve greatness in anything, countless difficult and painful attempts are often a prerequisite to be good at what one loves to do with their life.

Out of the blue, all my memories with friends, professors, classmates and past relationship partners came whooshing in my mind. Nostalgia crept up inside me as I felt my eyes well up. I was happy, sad, relieved, scared, proud and grateful at the same time.

I approached my support group who were all smiles and cheers – my mom, Jackson, Andy and Laura. We took countless pictures that would end up in picture frames, albums and social media. My mother looked so proud of me and I was happy to see her be there, watching me accomplish a life achievement.

At the corner of my eyes, I caught a glimpse of the person I was so lucky to meet at the University. A man so generous, kind and understanding. A man who helped me in so many ways. He helped me grow as a person and believed in me without a doubt.

The one who got away.

Jason was talking with his parents, I assumed, given their age gap and physical resemblance. I approached him to say 'hello' or maybe bid my 'final goodbye'.

"Hi Jason!" I said trying to sound cheery.

Jason turned around to face me as he lit up in a warm smile.

"Hello Emma. Congratulations!" He didn't hesitate to give me a big hug. I was bemused for a moment but I tried to act casual as though I wasn't feeling an explosion of delight inside.

"Thanks! Congrats to you too! So, what's next for you?" I said on impulse.

"I'm working on a startup with a business partner. What about you?" He held my gaze for a moment.

"Just playing it by ear" I downplayed my plans because I got none. I pressed my lips together to halt myself from saying more.

"I see, if you ever need help —"

"Oh there you are! Sorry it took me a while to find the restroom!" Chimed in a petite brunette who flashed us a hearty smile.

She must be Jason's sister. She's got a pretty face and a bubbly personality. I gave her my most friendly and sincerest grin for good first impression.

"That's okay. Uhm... Kylie, this is Emma." Jason was staring at the girl looking a bit flushed.

"Hi, I'm Kylie. Jason's girlfriend." She shook my hand looking straight into my eyes. "Nice to meet you Emma! Congratulations for graduating! What's your field of study?" She said with much enthusiasm and delight.

It was all happening in slow motion. I was speechless in shock. I felt my cheeks puffing out resentfully. In fact, I wanted to shoot a blow dart on her neck when she looked up at Jason and gave him a suggestive come-hither smile in front of me. I was livid, my animal instinct wanted to fight her to death like a queen ant tearing her exoskeleton with my powerful ant jaws.

Then I came to my senses. Jason doesn't want me anymore. He'd moved on, but there I was thinking crazy thoughts about a nice girl I just met. I missed my chance to be with him, but I can still be his good friend. I'm officially an adult now. I just graduated for heaven's sake. I had to grow up and toughen up in the face of adversity. Even in heartbreak.

"Thank you. Communications. I have a Communications Degree." I said as politely as I could.

I looked back and saw my family waiting for me.

"Well, it was nice to meet you. I should be going back to my family. Good luck and take care."

I stepped backward, waved them goodbye then turned my stride away.

CHAPTER EIGHTEEN

Off to Paris

Mom and I had an afternoon tea in her quaint gazebo in the backyard surrounded by shrubs, vines and various shades of pink English roses. Spring was in full bloom as evident in the luscious greenery and blossoming flowers around us. The fresh scent of nature was relaxing, and the chirping of birds perched on top of trees was music to my ears. Mom had an earl grey tea with milk while I sipped on a calming chamomile tea.

I couldn't believe how easy it was to talk to my mom about anything under the sun. She listened to my silly shaggy-dog stories with much enthusiasm and vivacity. She laughed hysterically at my embarrassing anecdotes and sympathized with my thoughts of yearning, sadness and failures. Mom gave me her undivided attention as though I was the most important person she's ever talked to in her life. I wondered if she'd always been like that because if she was, I've surely missed out growing up with a loving and caring mother.

Finally, mom smiled at me and took a deep sigh.

"So tell me about what you're most excited about right now?" Mom beamed at me as she sipped her tea.

"Uhm, nothing much." I said sounding nonplussed.

"Can I help you with anything?" She looked into my eyes as though she could read my innermost thoughts and emotions.

"No, I'm fine, mom. Thank you."

Without saying anything more, my eyes confessed the secrets of my heart.

"Close your eyes for me, will you dear?" Mom said mildly, gazing at me with soulful eyes.

"Why? Are we playing hide and seek?" I muttered as I gave a snort of laughter.

With a dreamy smile, mom had a wistful expression. I gave in and slowly closed my eyes as I felt the refreshing spring breeze blowing on my face.

"You're in a safe place where you won't be judged by anyone." Her voice was calming and hypnotic as though she's a psychotherapist.

"Imagine yourself being in a place where you've always wanted to go. Where would that be?" Mom's quiet voice was gentle and warmhearted.

"Why do you want to know, mom?" I said inquisitively, trying to stay calm as I kept my eyes tightly closed.

"Because I want to know more about my lovely daughter. Think of me as your confidante. Just relax, breathe... and let your thoughts wander. I'm here to listen." She was silent for a long while which made me feel reposeful. I breathed in and breathed out. In a few moments, I was feeling restful and calm.

"What's the place you've always wanted to go?" Mom slowly muttered forbearingly.

"I... I wish I'd be able to go to Paris one day. I've only seen it in photos and movies, and I've read books about it. I'd like to wander around, sip coffee or wine by the sidewalk patio as I watch strangers pass by. I'd love to just get lost in that beautiful city." I let out a dreamy smile with my eyes still shut.

"That's wonderful, love. Paris is enchanting. You should experience it while you're still young." She paused for a moment. "And why Paris in particular?" Mom added mildly.

"I've been writing a romantic novel set in Paris for a few months now... I love it, mom! Writing is just so freeing! But I think it'll be helpful if I see Paris in the flesh one day."

"Is that what you love doing? Writing?"

I felt the crisp wind in my hair as though I was floating in the sky. Then I took a deep breath of the sweet, soft fresh scent of blossoms in the garden. It had to be the most peaceful state I've ever been.

"Yeah, I would love to be a writer. Since I was a child, I could easily make up bizarre stories in my head. These ideas just come to me when I least expect them. They're like ghosts staying for a visit without notice. The only fair thing to do is to give them life on someone else's imagination. I'd like to write interesting stories for the rest of my life!"

I felt a sudden rush of clarity inside me. It was as though I was certain of what I desired in life all along. I knew my gift and purpose from the start, but I never trusted myself that I'd be good enough. I just thought it would be too hard.

I slowly pried my eyes open, and I was almost blinded by the brightness of the colorful, enchanting garden on a nice spring afternoon. My eyes had been closed in total darkness for far too long.

Beauty surrounded us, and I was sitting across my mother whom I never knew for the past twenty-three years. But there she was, listening intently to my deepest, innermost thoughts. From that moment on, she knew me better than anyone else.

"Emma, my love... You are a writer. The most important thing is that you know *why* you are doing what you love to do. You are one hundred percent in control of your life. You might as well use your time doing things that *fulfill* you and make you *feel alive*."

I smiled at mom as we faced each other in the sliver of sunshine that beamed over the gazebo. I felt absolutely weightless. Being with her lifted my spirits on cloud nine. Her words were like waves of relief rippling down my spine.

"Would you let me read what you've written so far?" Mom's voice was tender and soft. Her face was a perfect picture of tranquility.

"Okay, mom." I touched her arm affectionately.

Out of the blue, as though one of the ghosts had come and visited me at the moment, a thought crystallized in my mind.

"Let me play you a song in my ukulele!" With quick moving feet, I dashed inside the house and looked for my tiny instrument I brought along for our weekend entertainment.

"This is for you, mom!" I felt a surge of giddiness as I held my small four-stringed instrument.

I gently closed my eyes and started strumming *Claire de Lune.* I was one with the music, the wind and the sun as I played the melody that made my heart peel like petals. I felt love, sadness, hope, and exhilaration all at once.

"Would you stay for a couple more days?" Mom grabbed hold of my hand and fixed me with a wistful gaze. "I'd love for you to continue writing while you're here. It will bring me so much joy to read your novel while the story unfolds."

I stared at mom in bewilderment. I felt excited to get started writing. She believed in me. She inspired me to keep working on my dream.

"Yes, of course mom. I'll stay for a couple more days." I flashed her a wide smile with a twinkle in my eye.

I kept writing for hours. My mind was in full concentration. Scenes flashed before my eyes as I wrote them. I've gotten to know my characters on a deeper level as though they confided with me their truest desires and taunting fears. I've sympathized with them at their worst and revered them at their best. At the end of each day, I submitted my finished work to mom with pride and joy. It was as if I was unstoppable. I felt like I was on top of the world! I was writing for my most important reader — my mother. I wanted her to see me in my glory, showing her what I was capable of. I didn't care if nobody else would like what I've written, I've longed for my mother to be proud of me doing what I loved the most.

Mom was very supportive as she brought me food and beverage in my room. She gave me kisses on my forehead every time she checked up on me. I was like a spoiled child who got dinner served in her bedroom because she was too cool to come down to join the rest of the family for dinner. I used up all the time I've got staying at mom's place to write. When my extended stay was over, I completed three chapters. It was far more than what I've accomplished in four months. It was as if I knew my time there would be over soon, so I've harnessed all of my creativity in such a short period of time.

I packed my bags to go back home to my apartment. I was over the moon for accomplishing a lot during my stay in mom's house. She had definitely changed me. She was my mentor, my confidante, my *spiritual guru.*

"Before you go, I have a little something for you." Mom passed me an envelope with a bunch of papers in it. I ran my eyes through them, scanning what they're for. My whole body stiffened in shock.

My eyes widened like a deer in the headlights. "*Trip to Paris?!* Mom, I can't—"

I wavered as I cried like a baby and threw my arms around her. She gazed at me and pulled a thoughtful face.

"Go and experience Paris!" Mom held me tightly and kissed me like a little five year-old child who's going to see Disneyland for the very first time.

"Mom, this is too much... I don't deserve this!" My throat gradually tightened as I wiped the tears streaming down my face.

"Yes, you do, my love. You deserve to experience the greatest moment of your life while you're still young. I've never been there for you when you were growing up. I've missed twenty-three years of your life. This is the least I can do to make it up to you." Mom swallowed hard as her eyes started welling up too.

Mom had been organizing my trip for the past two days when I succumbed myself to writing like a madman. She conspired with Andy to book my flight to Paris. My accommodation was taken care of. I'd be staying at my mother's friend's apartment in Paris. She also included a check for me to cash in as my pocket money for the trip. I'd be staying in Paris for a week. It was like I won the lottery!

"Mom, this flight is three days from today... and in *business class*?!" I said with a pang of excitement inside me.

"Yes, love. You better start packing." Mom leaned forward and hugged me heartily.

There I was on an airplane soaring over the clouds with a glass of champagne as I wrote my animated thoughts of what's to come in just a few hours. Anticipation kept me awake the entire flight across new time zones.

Time flew by as I found myself in *Charles de Gaulle* airport. I was really in *Paris*. In the blink of an eye, my dream of coming to Paris came true. With one suitcase in hand, I stopped in the middle of a bustling walkway. I looked around for a moment as I pinched my arm just to make sure I wasn't dreaming.

I took a cab to get to Paris' city center. I opened the car window and as I looked up, my heart skipped a beat. I fell in love with Paris' beauty. My mouth parted in shock whilst my eyes widened in awe. The intricately designed lampposts. The elegant dark green Metro signs, water fountains and benches. The opulent Haussmannian apartments in palettes of blue and cream. The grand bridges, canals and boulevards. Everywhere I looked seemed like a museum filled with grandiosity. I couldn't snap out of my reverie. I've never seen anything like it. It was even more beautiful than what I've expected it to be.

The driver dropped me off at the apartment I was staying in near Notre Dame Cathedral. It was a cream-colored building with ornate balconies with flowers in bloom. I stood in front of a wooden royal blue giant doorway. It was intricately carved with a gold door knocker designed with Zeus' face. It felt like I was facing the entryway to *Narnia*. I was welcomed by the apartment caretaker, and I had the entire place all to myself.

"Bonjour, Emma!" He greeted me jovially extending his arm to shake my hands. "I'm Maxime!

"Bonjour, Monsieur Maxime!" I said with pride practicing my French greeting.

"Good flight?" He asked, turning his head to face me as he lifted my carry-on suitcase.

"Yes, it was." I let out a wide grin although I was feeling jetlagged.

We got inside the main entrance hallway with high ceilings, paneled with huge mirrors on either side. Maxime led me all the way to the courtyard — a lovely and quaint private garden surrounded by the entire building where tenants could watch you from above like gladiators in the *Colosseum*. Maxime took out a humongous *1800s* brass skeleton key from his pocket to open the apartment building's metal door entrance. I thought he was joking when he dangled them in front of my face because they looked like jail keys to the bastille. Maxime said my apartment was on the fourth floor, which was technically on the fifth floor *if you're from North America*. There was a charming wide spiral staircase going up. There was no elevator in the building but that was perfectly fine because it somehow made my experience much more authentic.

When we got to the fourth floor, Maxime led me to a large wooden door that he opened with the other brass skeleton key. We got inside the apartment, which was opulent, cozy and clean. I had a plush queen-sized bed with fresh white linens, a posh bathroom and a fully stocked kitchen. I had everything I needed in my temporary abode. I could leave or come home whenever I pleased. I had total freedom and it was perfect. I thanked Maxime for his warm hospitality. He gave me some tourist tips and recommended some places to eat out.

My body surrendered to the soft bed with plush warm blankets after brushing my teeth and taking a refreshing shower. I decided to take a ten-minute nap before I'd be ready to head out and start strolling around. I've anticipated sitting on a red cane bistro chair in the patio watching interesting characters pass by as I sip on another glass of champagne, *s'il vous plait.*

I overslept. I stopped the snooze button for ten minutes and ended up dozing off for six hours. It was already evening and I was starving. The sun was still out so it didn't seem like I've wasted precious hours in Paris sleeping.

I found an olde bistro right outside the apartment building. I sat down and a lovely elderly gentleman came to my table as I greeted him with '*bonjour*' but he politely responded with '*bonsoir*' since it was already evening. I realized the difference without any translation. There was a menu written in French on a small blackboard with three options. Having no idea of what they were, I asked the charming elderly bistro owner if he could translate. He responded to me in French so I nodded with a smile and pointed at the first option on the board. I then added the word *champagne* to which he affirmed with delight. I crossed my fingers and hoped that I ordered something appetizing. Pointing to words I didn't understand with no pictures for reference was quite exciting. *Come what may. Surprise me.*

I was very pleased that I've actually ordered a cheese platter with salami and prosciutto that paired perfectly with my fizzy beverage of choice. I was sitting right next to the sidewalk with a table approximately two feet in diameter as I watched pedestrians pass me by. I finished my supper and started walking aimlessly. I followed the Seine River until it led me to where lots of people flock by. The walkways were filled with locals drinking bottles of wine and smoking cigarettes laissez-faire style. The tourist boats sailed endlessly along the river. I wandered aimlessly taking thousands of pictures to preserve my memories of the city.

It was dark and late at night and the city was still filled with people walking on the sidewalks and the roads were busy with heaps of vehicles driving by. I've reached the top of the Pont Alexander III bridge where I found a heart-stopping view of the Eiffel Tower glimmering with its golden lights.

I've made it. I'm here. I'm living my dream. Tears were streaming down my cheeks. At that moment, my heart was filled with pure joy and peace. I've never felt so lucky to be alive.

CHAPTER NINETEEN

Rendezvous with a Stranger

I woke up early and headed straight to a *boulangerie,* a local bakery in France. I picked up a freshly baked baguette and a cup of coffee while I strolled my way through the banks of Seine River. I gazed at the heart-stopping view of Notre Dame Cathedral beaming with the rays of a Parisian sunrise at the morning golden hour. I found the perfect spot to sit where I dangled my feet over the water as I read the sensational Paris memoir of Ernest Hemingway, *A Moveable Feast.*

Hemingway was part of the famous bohemian culture of the expatriate community of genius artists and writers in the 1920's called, *The Lost Generation.* He wrote about his long walks all over Paris that gave him inspiration to write. He frequented this charming bookstore called *Shakespeare and Company.* He recounted memories of himself walking along Seine River and Luxembourg Gardens. He used to write for hours at a café in Place St.-Michel with his usual rounds of café au lait, rum or wine. Hemingway wrote about Paris like it was a dreamland where artists and writers flocked to be inspired.

I felt incredibly excited to write. It was the only logical thing to do in a movie-like location for a romantic international indie film with witty dialogues and cinematic panning. I brought my fully charged laptop and started typing away until the bright sun was fully glinting on my face. I kept writing until I got hungry again. I desperately needed a cup of warm café crème so I crossed the bridge on foot and let myself get lost in the 4th arrondissement. The fancy shops and restaurants oozed with vibrant energy as I strolled around the uber chic neighborhood of Le Marais. Charming antique shops, restaurants, vintage clothing stores and cafés lined the neighborhood's narrow streets.

I strode down a random alley and found a row of bicycles parked on the side of the road. I caught a glimpse of myself in the glass windows of Le Peloton Café.

The coffee shop was small but very inviting with a warm atmosphere. The staff were English-speaking friendly expats. A tall blonde lady promptly served my café crème and scrumptious waffles with strawberries and powdered sugar. I gorged on my second breakfast like a true-blood starving artist who just completed a weeklong intermittent fasting.

After a good five minutes, I looked up feeling pleasantly satisfied as though it was my last meal on death row. A guy from the next table wearing a black jacket seemed genuinely fascinated looking at me. He had a dreamy smile with deep dimples denting both of his cheeks. I shot him a curious look feeling a bit self-conscious as I scratched the itch on my neck.

He pointed on his nose then pointed at me.

What is this, Simon says? He's cute but a little too eccentric for my taste.

I tried to ignore his weird gesticulations, but he kept waving at me from his table.

I pretended to check my phone instead and acted like I got a text message.

I nearly fell off my chair as I saw the reflection of my own face.

Great, I have a significant amount of white powder on my nose like a coke addict.

The powdered sugar looked very convincing. *I could have been a double for Tony Montana in Scarface when he snorted a heap of his own supply dazed in the highest form of karmic bliss. It was Oscar-worthy.*

I mouthed *'Thanks'* at him feeling awkwardly shamefaced as I wiped off the faux cocaine with the unused surface of my crumpled napkin.

I took a lady-like sip of my coffee to recover from my unrefined demeanor. As I slowly looked up, I met his bluish grey eyes beaming a look of wonderment. I felt a slight flush come to my cheeks as I tucked my hair behind my ear exposing the palm of my hand. I guess that was my modern take to the uncanny eighteenth century fan flirting.

I was possibly attempting to have my first Paris flirtation with a handsome stranger. He got up from his seat then pushed his chair back. He was about to leave.

I should at least try to get his name or say something profoundly impressive in French! What are the words I could say in French? Think... Quickly!

I looked up and made eye contact with him as I mindlessly uttered, "Bonjour! Excusez-moi, les toilettes?"

Why the heck did I ask him where the restroom is.

To my surprise, he stopped right in front of me and said; "I think the restroom's over there," pointing to the sign that says "La Toilette" hanging visibly for everyone to see under an intricately designed metal bracket. He spoke in a soft, patient voice but looked at me wryly. I was either high on caffeine or his deep blue grey eyes just penetrated my soul. Or both.

"Merci Beaucoup!" I was grinning ear to ear when I tipped over my coffee cup like a clumsy dork finally talking to her crush at the school cafeteria. A few drops of leftover caffeine stained my crisp white long sleeved shirt.

Now I really have to go to the restroom but I'm just going to play it cool this time with a flirty side-glance.

I took some paper towel and wetted it with water and a dollop of hand soap. I got carried away scrubbing all of my life's frustrations off my shirt. It kind of worked in removing most of the stain but now I had a huge wet spot on my left boob, and it looked like I was a lactating mother of three.

Great, of course there's no hand dryer.

I walked out of the restroom with one arm covering my soaked left bosom.

As I walked back, I noticed *Mr. Milky Way Eyes* sitting across my table as though he was waiting for me. I found myself not minding this peculiar situation at all because I had a crush on him. Otherwise, it would have been downright creepy.

As though he can feel my gaze, he looked back at my direction and beamed at me.

"I stayed to watch over your stuff while you were gone."

"Thank you. You didn't have to do that." His eyes met mine once more as I felt my face tingling slightly.

"I wanted to. I'm Damien."

"Emma."

I sat down across him nodding my head awkwardly. I was mesmerized by his presence like I was under some kind of a voodoo love spell.

"Let me get you another cup of coffee."

He added as I opened my mouth, "Café crème, right?"

"How did you know?" I said in my most jovial voice.

"It's a pretty small place. I overheard what you ordered earlier. Traveling solo?"

"Yes, my first time ever."

The freshly brewed cuppa came sooner than I'd anticipated. My caffeine concoction stimulated my excitement at each sip.

"Do you need a tour guide?" Damien fixed his eyes on mine with charming dimples defining his enticing smile.

"Do you live in Paris?" I rested my elbows on the table and cupped my face with the palm of my hand.

"No, I arrived here yesterday. I'll be leaving the city in a few days."

"Well, how much do you charge?" I heard myself say in an attempt to have a casual café flirtation.

Damien shook his head in mock disapproval.

"For you, absolutely nothing."

I took a deep breath and gave him my best teasing look. "Nothing's ever free."

"It is... with me." He said with a smirk while he took another sip of his drink.

Staring at him in bewilderment, I began to feel a little hot under his gaze. He seemed mysterious and innocent at the same time. He was a handsome, tall, blonde stranger with eyes as blue as the ocean.

"C'mon, you gotta have at least pictures that weren't taken as selfies right? We're just gonna be a couple of strangers walking around and doing random stuff. It'll be fun!"

"Well, you're right about the pictures. I kind of need at least one hero shot to show off back home. But is it worth getting murdered by a possible serial killer?" I said crossly.

"Probably not. But what if I'm not a serial killer but just a harmless guy who wants to wander around Paris with a beautiful stranger?" He said casually.

"Prove it." I said with a little laugh. "Prove you're not a psycho."

"We can stay here for another half an hour and if you still have that gut feeling that I am in any way a danger to your safety, then run. In the meantime, let me take a cute photo of you to demonstrate my photography skills." He pulled out his phone to snap a quick picture of me.

I stuck my tongue out and crossed my eyes like an awkward weirdo. He showed me the picture and kept it despite my juvenile attempt to look like a legitimate problem child at the daycare.

After consuming a whole bottle of wine and another round of coffee later, we lost track of the time talking for three hours straight. I told him about my heartbreak stories and my simple life philosophy in traveling and writing. He shared his own past love affairs and his current job at an oil rig in the Gulf of Mexico. Hours passed and we both felt like we've known each other for years.

Damien and I walked around the streets of Paris that night. We ended up at the banks of Seine River where cool locals hang out to drink as endless rounds of tourist boats passed by. We had a lovely spontaneous picnic by the river with artisanal cheese, baguette and a bottle of champagne.

Damien lit a cigarette and effortlessly inhaled smoke into his lungs like a popular cool, bad boy trope from a cheesy blockbuster teen movie. I watched him blow the smoke out as he slowly turned his head to face me. He caught me staring at his handsome face admiring him with my mouth slightly parted. I was having a major crush on a stranger I just met a few hours ago.

The way he held his cigarette in between his fingers. The charming lines on his face when he smiles. His sparkling deep blue-grey eyes tearing up as he burst out laughing uncontrollably. His low soothing voice and hypnotizing nods when he talks. There's something so mesmerizing about him.

Curious about what it was like to be onboard the tourist boats along the Seine River at night, we bought two tickets on a whim. I've come to a conclusion that Paris is even more beautiful at night. The majestic architectural buildings were illuminated in the dark. We had the best romantic view of the Eiffel Tower at the top deck of the boat.

My jaw dropped as I looked up at the most emblematic monument in the world, dancing with glimmering lights right in front of us. The Eiffel Tower's beauty was entrancing. I finally made it. I was there. I saw it in the flesh and there was nothing more that I could have ever asked for at that moment.

"So beautiful." Damien whispered in my ear.

"Have you ever seen anything... more enchanting than this?" I murmured slowly, turning to face him. "It's perfect, isn't it?"

"Yes... I think I'm bewitched." Damien laid his eyes on me and gradually moved his gaze from my eyes to my lips. He gently leaned closer and landed his soft lips against mine. I slowly shut my eyes as I felt a slight pang inside.

I didn't want that moment to end. I opened my eyes bit by bit. He was gazing at me only a few inches away.

"What have you done to me, Emma?" He was staring at me while shaking his head with a dreamy simper on his face.

"Could you promise me one thing?" I mumbled teasingly.

"Promise you what?"

"Promise me you won't have a crush on me." I exclaimed, my face was flushing as I let out a little laugh.

Damien gave an explosive snort of laughter.

"Whatever, pinky promise?" I said with a little shrug as I stuck out my little finger.

"No dice. I don't make promises I can't keep." He bestowed a charming smile on me and followed it with a boyish wink. He kissed me passionately one more time. When our lips parted, I let out a breath that sounded like a lustful moan. He gave me a teasing smile and shook his head knowingly.

"Well, maybe I should be the one warning you not to have a crush me!" Damien ran his fingers on my cheeks like a sculptor studying his masterpiece.

"Not a chance." I joshed.

The boat made its way back to the dock and we were the only ones left sitting on the top deck like deluded lovebirds who got lost in migration. I took a deep breath and stared at his face incredulously. I just had the most romantic night in Paris with a beautiful stranger.

The next day, I met up with Damien for breakfast. We had some freshly brewed café allongé and sumptuous avocado toasts. We didn't have any plans but when the caffeine kicked in, we decided to hop on a train and check out *Versailles*. Just an hour ride from Paris, we've reached the famous grand palace. It was opulent, extravagant and lavish inside and out. There were endless rooms and hallways decorated with gold leaves, gilded historical paintings and crystal chandeliers. After an hour of wandering around massive bedrooms of French monarchs, we've decided to venture into the other parts of the palace.

We walked towards the famous Hall of Mirrors. The ballroom walls were surrounded by a ludicrous number of mirrors, chandeliers, sculptures and vaulted ceilings with paintings depicting France's war victories. To say that everything was over the top was an understatement. After a while, I've gotten blasé about the sight of gigantic historical portraits of powerful, wealthy people staring down at modern-day peasants like me.

Fortunately, I saw a huge open window from one of the balconies that provided a bird's eye view of Versailles' crowning glory — its massive breathtaking manicured gardens. My eyes had never been graced with so much greenery and intricate architecture.

Damien came right up behind me and planted his left hand on my waist as he looked at the garden surveying the beauty of this man-made paradise. It was a lovely sunny day with clear blue skies. I looked up at him while squinting in the glare of the sun. He drew a deep breath and flashed me an earnest smile with glimmering eyes. He leaned closer to me and stole a kiss on my cheek.

"I like you, Emma. I'm happy to be here with you." Damien wrapped his arms around me while we stood on the palace's balcony gazing over what felt like heaven on earth.

I was lost of words to say. I just held onto him tightly as he squeezed my body closer to his. Damien gently took my hand and kissed it like a dashing handsome prince from a fairytale. Waves of jitters rippled down my spine. We were acting like a couple of escaped insane asylum patients who were crazy for each other.

Pretending to be old-time lovers walking hand in hand, we perused the luscious discreet groves closed off by walls of greenery and trellises. I teased Damien by running away in the middle of our passionate kiss.

"You could kiss me some more if you catch me." I slowly took a couple of steps backing away from him then I dashed as fast as I could.

It didn't take too much effort for Damien to grab me by the waist and kissed me intensely in a secret garden far from the swarms of unsuspecting tourists. Our trance was abruptly interrupted by a little cute boy staring at us as we made out in Apollo's Bath Grove. Behind him were both his grandparents trying to capture his photograph with high-powered optical zoom, I'm sure.

We discovered docked rowboats for rent as we passed by the lake. Blokes were obliged to paddle as a gentlemanly act of chivalry for their beloveds. It was an idealistic royal rendezvous that was just too hard to pass for suckers like us.

"How's your rowing skills?" I asked while I slightly touched Damien's arm.

"I guess we'll find out." He said with a crooked boyish grin on his face.

Passing clouds above us covered the lake. It made our vantage point of the palace's perimeter a lot more comfortable without squinting under the bright rays of the sun. I felt the wind in my hair as I marveled at the romantic view of the Grand Palace of Versailles. Damien stopped rowing when we reached the middle. He took a deep breath and closed his eyes. Then he drained all the air from his lungs with much satisfaction.

"I've never felt more peaceful. This is nice." He looked around taking in the majestic view.

The royal residence of the French monarchs with its intricate manicured gardens felt like a dreamy setting for a period piece Hollywood film.

"You're beautiful." I heard him whisper.

Damien's words made me feel a sudden prickle of nervousness in my stomach.

"Did you say that so I'd take the turn to row the boat?" I bantered.

"Absolutely! Here, take the paddles!" He retorted back with a little laugh.

Damien and I came back to Paris late in the afternoon. Before the sun had set that day, we got to Sacré-Cœur Basilica atop the Montmartre hill. It was a gleaming white domed edifice that sat on the highest point of the city. We secured a spot in the crowded stairs where we drank cold beers sold by unrelenting peddlers roaming around. We gasped in admiration watching the rays of light gradually bid goodbye with the golden sunset. Then before we even realized, Paris was transformed into the City of Lights.

At the back of the basilica was the café-laden square of Place du Tertre. Romantic bistros glowed with warm lights. This village-like place was filled with charming cobblestone pathways and Bohemian souvenir shops selling trinkets and memorabilia.

A hypnotizing jazzy music drew us to *La Crémaillère 1900*. A beautiful, elegant Parisian lady singing and playing the piano set the mood for our romantic Parisian date night. She was lodged in a mini platform stage playing the gleaming black grand piano for patrons' entertainment. Her ivory skin contrasted stunningly with her rouge lips and onyx hair pulled up in a polished

French chignon bun. Her body was draped with a sparkly black long-sleeved dress that hugged her curves like a Greek goddess. We couldn't resist her presence. She was captivating.

Damien ordered a bottle of Pinot Noir. We feasted on escargot and frog legs for appetizers, beef bourguignon and confit de canard for the main course. For dessert, crème brûlée of course. The skies were dark and the crescent moon was subtly peeking from above. But the illuminating lights from the streetlamps set the mood for a sultry Paris romance.

An artist offered to have our portraits done while we sip our wines and watch people walk by in the outside patio of the restaurant. We said yes. It was an honor, really. *How many people could say they've been to Paris and got their portraits drawn by a legitimate French artist?* He wasn't wearing a beret but he was an older gentleman who seemed to have had decades of experience producing express portraits of strangers even at night.

About half an hour later, Damien and I had a hand-drawn sketched portrait of us together. It was an image of a young couple with a glint of deranged infatuation in their eyes. His impression of our physical hysteria about each other was surreal. We had that magical moment preserved by another stranger.

Paris' nightlife won't be as authentic without chain smoking and binge-drinking. We've been to a couple of kooky speakeasy bars. One was hidden behind a laundromat's commercial washing machine and the other was tucked behind a faux mini-grocery store shelf filled with Nutella and Campbell's soup. These hidden bars accommodate about a maximum of thirty people. We felt like we were part of an underground group exchanging philosophical thoughts and ground-breaking ideas that could spark a revolution. Their bohemian atmosphere was filled with throw pillows for floor seats and rattan hanging egg chairs. But it must have been the continuous flow of alcohol in our system or the pent-up lustful desire we've been concocting all day that made us decide to go hurrying home like horny gorillas.

Damien called a cab and our make out session started in the poor cab driver's backseat. It seemed like time flew by when we arrived in front of my apartment building. Endless flights of spiral staircase later, we finally got inside my bedroom. There was still leftover white wine in the fridge that I've saved from a day ago. We alternately sipped from the bottle. Then Damien carried me to bed just a few steps away and gently laid me in the cloud of satin pillows and linen sheets. The only light we had was the glint of the moonlight shining through the lofty glass windows of the room.

His breathing tickled my skin. Each kiss initiated irrepressible moans as we caressed each other's whims and desires. It felt like a forbidden night. A tryst that may or may not lead up to a heartache the next day. Damien and I both knew our time together was imminent to end.

He slowly unbuttoned my blouse to reveal my bosom wide open for his surveying eyes. I did not hesitate to lift his shirt as I ran my hands through his firm and strong arms. He proceeded to unzip my pants as he traced kisses from my stomach all the way down in between my legs. It was a surreal form of ecstasy – it felt like I was taken into another dimension as my legs shook while he planted sucking kisses in my innermost sensibilities. I returned the favor and caressed his manhood while I bit on my lower lip to show him my unquenchable desire. He let out a lustful moan as I traced my mouth to where he was craving to be touched. Just about when he could not take the surge of erotic bliss anymore, I climbed on top of him to ride his manhood until we both collapsed into a climax of pure carnal pleasure.

We made love half a dozen times from dusk 'till noon the next day. I succumbed to his irresistible charm. Damien was a sex god. Needless to say, he satiated my undiagnosed erotic reservations. By late afternoon the next day, we were holding each other under the covers as though we have confined ourselves to a lifetime of mushy cuddling.

"I really like you... This is bad." Damien took a deep breath and tightened his grip around my arms. I rested my head over his chest and kissed it slowly, working my way up to his cheeks and finally to his lips. I couldn't stop myself from looking at him.

I wanted to keep the memory of him whenever I needed to be happy again. Meeting him was like finding a treasure I couldn't keep. He was perfect. Or at least that memory of us together in the sliver of time. And it shall be so, forever in my mind.

Damien took me to the historical Crémerie-Restaurant Polidor where the likes of Ernest Hemingway, Victor Hugo and Arthur Rimbaud were once regular patrons. Its charming interior spoke of old world Paris with long tables shared with other diners like we were in a French grandma's house waiting for her delicious home-cooked meals. The escargot, foie gras, beef bourguignon and supreme poulet were all unpretentiously sensational with their house red wine. The restroom situation was quite dated as though they were straight from the 1800's. It was as simple as a hole in the floor. But to be honest, I wouldn't have preferred it any other way.

It was our last day together. Damien held my hand the entire night as we made our way back to my apartment. My flight back home was the next day. I didn't want to leave. I was living my dream life in my 'dream city' and making out with my 'dream guy'. Soon I'd have to wake up to reality.

We stopped in front of the entrance door of my apartment building. It was probably wise that he didn't come up or it would have been another sleepless night.

"I'd like to meet you for breakfast tomorrow at Le Peloton Café before you leave." Damien lifted my hand and kissed it gently.

"My flight will be at noon. See you there at eight o'clock?" I threw my hands around him like a vulnerable child.

"Of course, my flight won't be until late night tomorrow. I could take you to the airport."

"You promise?" I raised my little finger to him as though it was the only way I would have assurance that he would.

"I won't let you go without saying goodbye." Damien intertwined his pinky with mine.

"Good, cause if you don't show up... I'll cry." A faint of wistfulness was evident in my face.

I knew it was not yet the end. I was still going to see him the next day before I flew back home. But something in me just didn't want to let him go at that moment. His arms encircled mine and he held me as tightly as he could. I looked up at his face and his gaze flicked toward me. There was a momentary silence between us. I could have stood there by the street kissing him passionately all night. Instead, we stared at each other in quiet melancholy as though we were at the end of the road.

"I'll see you tomorrow at eight o'clock." Damien stepped back as he put his hands in his pockets.

"I'll be there." I said as I turned my back to get inside my apartment building.

I closed the enormous door behind me. I drew a deep breath and reminded myself that I would still see him one last time the next day.

I got to Le Peloton Café exactly at eight o'clock in the morning with my suitcase in hand. I only slept for three hours mostly because I wrote Damien a hand-written letter that night. I've been waiting for twenty minutes. Damien was late so I ordered my last café crème in Paris. I resisted the urge to order food until Damien got there since I wanted to eat breakfast with him.

I was getting worried when he still hadn't showed up. It was forty-five minutes after eight o'clock and I had to leave soon to get to the airport.

Because Damien and I had been inseparable for days, we haven't even exchanged phone numbers. He took several pictures of me but we didn't have any pictures together. We have not talked about connecting on any social media or thought of giving each other our addresses in case we wanted to be at least pen pals. I didn't even know his last name. Why had I not thought about all this information before our last day?

I felt my facade was beginning to crumble. I waited for an hour, but Damien was a no-show. I had to make a calculated decision, or I wouldn't make it onboard my flight back home.

There it was in my hand. My letter to Damien I wrote all night. I scribbled all of my contact information at the back of the paper in a rush. Physical address, phone number, email and all my social media accounts. I handed my letter to the café server and explained that I was supposed to meet someone, but I had to leave given my situation. I showed her our sketched portrait together and she took a picture of it on her phone so she could remember his face if he ever shows up at the cafe.

I left her a huge tip and begged her to relay my message and letter. I felt a little thrill of trepidation. I stood outside the café for a few more minutes one last time imagining Damien running frantically towards me as he lifted me up and spun me around like how it usually ends in a cliché rom-com movie.

But he never came. Tears of disappointment trickled down my cheeks as I drew a deep breath and started walking away with a suitcase rolling behind me. I didn't even have a slight inkling that he wouldn't show up. I thought it could still be one of those *'lad desperately running after a damsel in the middle of a crowded street'* situation. But there was still no Damien in sight. I was just a lone maniac stopping and looking back, interrupting busy pedestrians going about their merry way.

My flight back home left right on schedule. As the plane took off the ground, I wished that Damien eventually showed up at the café and got my letter. I may never know what happened to him that day. Maybe he woke up late. Maybe he decided not to show up at all. Maybe something really bad happened. Or maybe the universe made sure we were never going to see each other again. We both knew that our time together had an expiration date but that made it all more poignant. I really wished he had read my letter. Because he would have known that I had completely ignored his warning.

As crazy as it sounds, I might have fallen for a handsome stranger I met at a quaint little café in Le Marais.

CHAPTER TWENTY

Back to Reality

My airplane window seat gave me a last-minute bird's eye view of Paris amongst the clouds. I smiled to myself in disbelief of how lucky I was to have experienced it. My reverie took me to Paris' manicured gardens, cobble-stoned streets, cozy cafés, stately museums and laissez faire lifestyle. I got lost in its boulevards and avenues, but I'd never even been slightly bothered. I was happy to have experienced so much beauty all around me on my own. But the City of Love also paved a way for my short-lived love affair. I felt total freedom to be adventurous. To be myself. I've never felt more alive. *And for that, I'll always have Paris to bring magic in my heart.*

The seatbelt sign was turned off and we were flying at thirty thousand feet in the air. I took out my laptop to continue writing my novel. A couple more glasses of wine and six trips to the lavatory later, I kept writing for seven hours straight. I was tired and sleep-deprived but there could have been no other peaceful place to get lost in my own world than to be in a packed aircraft flying across continents with complete strangers. That was one of those moments when the fairy-godmother of creativity paid me a visit and I had to draw off every drop of inspiration while I was in her presence. I was in the zone. Crying babies, blabbering gossip and an infirm neighbor did not faze me. It could have been being stuck in the sky, the vino, or the fact that I've just had the time of my life in the most beautiful city in the world that got me excited to work even without sleep. *This must be what it feels like when people say, 'Do something you love and you'll never work a day in your life.' Or something certified workaholics say like, 'I'll sleep when I die!'*

When the plane landed back home, I was momentarily dumbfounded. It was immensely different from Paris. I've missed my small apartment. I felt like I've changed somehow, now that I've seen beauty outside my bubble.

There was a certain shift in my brain that made me notice and appreciate beauty around me. All of a sudden, I was interested to check out my city's heritage buildings, park gardens, local museums and upcoming festivals. My life was boring because I didn't try to look for interesting places, activities and people. It was only when I was in another country where I had no choice but to stop and smell the roses that I had an epiphany of how oblivious I was of my surroundings. Yes, it's not Paris. But now, everywhere I looked, I saw a picturesque background of a cinematic movie.

My taxi dropped me right in front of my apartment. I got out of the car, looked around and took a deep breath of spring right after a light rain. The driver must have thought I was filming a cheesy fabric softener commercial as my shoulders rose and dropped at a dramatic slow-mo pace. He took my luggage out of the trunk and waved me goodbye. I took my keys out and rolled my suitcase in the hallway of the building. Keys dangled in my hand as I slowly opened the doorknob to my humble abode. I was excited to see Andy!

"What the..." I was mortified to see so many rolls of fabric leaning against the wall, infinite cut pieces of cloth scattered on the floor and sewing pattern papers everywhere in the apartment.

Andy had his head resting down on the table with a portable sewing machine. It still had a silky red fabric fed in it. It looked like he passed out in the middle of sewing. I've never seen Andy that exhausted. I didn't have the heart to wake him up. He was so worn out, he didn't even hear that he was no longer alone inside our tiny apartment. I quietly made myself a cup of tea. The next best thing at that point was a good shower so I tiptoed my way to the bathroom to freshen up. Andy was snoring away in deep sleep. At least I had a clear indication that he's still alive.

I got out of the shower with a towel wrapped around me when I heard some movement. Andy was the best person to startle because he'd scream like he was being fed to the lions. I ducked against the wall and waited for the perfect opportunity to scare him as he approached the bathroom.

My timing couldn't have been perfect. I flipped my hair to the front of my face to look like a legitimate vindictive ghost from a well. I grabbed Andy's leg with my cold wet hands and made inaudible hoarse choking noise from my throat.

"Eeeekkkk! Crazy bitch!" Andy impulsively kicked me in the forehead. I rolled over the floor unravelling the tucked damp towel from my body.

Andy turned on the light screaming at the top of his lungs looking aghast. I flipped my hair back to witness the shock in his face while I burst out laughing.

"Oh my gawd, Emma! What in the holy ghost are you doing! I almost had an asthma attack!" Andy was breathing hard with two hands on his chest.

I forgot that I was fully naked whilst laughing like an annoying hyena. Andy pulled me up and threw the towel over me as he tried to contain the disgust in his face.

"What's wrong? Don't you like what you see?" I joshed, re-wrapping the towel in my chest.

"Frankly, No." He retorted barely missing a beat. "I'm not into naked, leg-grabbing demonic ghosts!" Andy grinned then gave me a big, warm bear hug.

"I see that you've turned our place into a sweatshop. Good job, now our landlord has reasonable grounds to finally evict us." I said with a little laugh as I wheeled around to face him.

He looked a bit disheveled and full of suppressed energy.

"Welcome to *House of Hawthorne*! See, I've been sketching designs, making patterns and sewing for days! Gawd, my back hurts! Look, this is my best work so far." Andy took an emerald silk evening gown from a shiny copper clothing rack stationed at the kitchen.

"Wow! This looks so glamorous! I didn't know you're this good!" I flicked back my wet hair and held the dress closer so I could inspect his masterpiece. The stitching was perfect, and the cut was sharp as if it was tailored by Gianni Versace himself. He could tell that I was very impressed.

"Thanks darling, well I've been designing and sewing clothes since the day I discovered that I wasn't really cut out to thrive in the pet food business." Andy's voice echoed confidence and charm.

"Yeah? When was that?"

"Since I was ten. Ed, you know, our butler? He taught me how to sew. I was trained by the best." There was a sting of pride in Andy's voice. It was evident that fashion was indeed his first and only love.

"I see a potential here, Hawthorne. You did good." My eyes lit up as I skimmed through his finished collection.

"So how was your trip? I need details... places you've seen, food you've eaten, and guys you've hooked up with. Go!" Andy walked to the fridge and took out a half-full bottle of red wine. He poured me a glass which meant that we were about to have a long overdue heart-to-heart talk.

"I met a guy... he was amazing..." I heard myself say out loud with a slight feeling of dismay.

"If he was so amazing, then why..." Andy came over and sat down beside me. "Oh no, honey! Did you fall in love with a stranger who may or may not have given you the best orgasm of your life?"

I looked at him in surprise. Andy might as well be the all-knowing Oracle from the Matrix.

"He's so kind, caring, romantic... And so handsome!" I said desperately.

"Ok, show me a picture!"

"I've got none on my phone, we didn't even take pictures together."

"What's his name? I'll look up his social media accounts!"

"Uhm, Damien. We're not linked up on any social media platform." I said reluctantly.

"Alright, what's Damien's last name?"

"Don't know."

"Okay, where does he live and what does he do for a living?"

"Somewhere in the Gulf of Mexico, drilling oil. I think."

"So do you see yourself meeting up with this guy again?"

I took a gulp of my wine avoiding eye contact with the head of Spanish inquisition.

"He stood me up. We were going to have breakfast together before I leave Paris but he was a no-show."

"How long have you been with this guy?" Andy gave me a quizzical look.

"Best three days of my life!" I blurted out feeling a slight swell of indignation.

"You've gone absolutely bonkers! He's just a vacation fling, darling. Why do you fret over someone you don't even know and will never ever see again?" Andy said, rolling his eyes.

"I think I might have fallen for him. He was perfect, Andy. I may never find another love like that!" I uttered haughtily as I took another sip from my glass.

"In three days?!" Andy shook his head ruefully then burst out laughing hysterically swinging the wine glass like a drunk evil clown.

I was going to defend my intense Paris love affair when my brain just clicked. He was right. It made no fucking sense. I had the fantasy of meeting my one true love who got away ala 'Before Sunrise' movie trope. Yes, I believe that I've met an amazing person who could have been "the one" but I may never ever meet him again in this lifetime. And I have to live with that. Because that's how life is. I had to accept the fact that one person I thought brought me a sliver of happiness was only meant to be in my life as a passing stranger. It was a fleeting moment that I could just keep in my 'feel-good' memories.

I smiled in relief. My eyes lit up in understanding as I nodded slowly staring at nothingness like The Enlightened one.

"Oh, actually Damien and I have a sketched portrait together by a French artist!" I recalled out of the blue whilst looking a bit dazed.

I tottered toward my suitcase to find the white sketch paper I carefully squished in my hand-carry luggage. Slowly, I unrolled it to reveal my ephemeral lover's sketch portrait.

Andy gazed at the sketch and said casually, "Well, that's you on the left alright! But you didn't say his face is kind of, well... melted."

I inspected the portrait and true enough, Damien's face looked like the melting wicked witch of the west. My travel size hand sanitizer leaked and drenched the paper portrait marring Damien's face as an unrecognizable blob of dried disinfected paper.

"Maybe it's a sign from the universe to just let him go. I mean, melted face?!" Andy looked at me wryly.

"It wasn't meant to be, and truthfully, I'm ok with that. He made my Paris trip even more memorable than I could ever imagine." I said with my head held high.

"So, no regrets?" Andy pried a little more.

"Regrets? Imagine all the stories I'll tell."

About the author

M.J. Amherst writes contemporary romance about messy love, complicated choices, and the moments that quietly shape who we become. Fascinated by the way relationships evolve through humor, heartbreak, and unexpected connection, she explores the delicate balance between passion and self-discovery in her stories.

When she isn't writing, she can usually be found people-watching in crowded cafés, filling notebooks with half-formed ideas, or planning her next trip somewhere that feels both unfamiliar and inspiring. She believes that love is rarely simple, growth is never linear, and the best stories are the ones that feel a little too real.